MW01126603

Cutthroat Chronicles: An Anthology of Deception
Copyright © 2018 by Free-Flo

ISBN **978-1987568899**

Printed in USA by CreateSpace (www.createspace.com)

Cutthroat Chronicles: An Anthology of Deception

Acknowledgements

Hebrew King

I would like to give thanks to my everything my strong fortress, my best friend, father and savior Yahuah esteem be to HE... I wanna send this shout out to my grandpa that just passed. I will forever carry your courage, boldness, toughness, loyalty, faith, and love with me wherever I go... I'm blessed for my family who has always allowed me to soar and be me. I thank all my true friends who never allowed me to settle for less or give up on my dreams. I thank you my Instagram family, Team Supreme. We are finally moving on up; y'all are the greatest!

To my son and my niece, NaNa, I truly thank you for always seeing the best in me even when I felt down and overwhelmed by the worldly views. I love y'all. I love all my nieces, nephews and lil cousins. All you play a part in my life. Y'all are my drive and inspiration. Shout out to my God-parents Kathy, John, and the Doss family. Without your love and guidance, I don't know what would've become of me when I was in Memphis. I love y'all dearly... I just wanna say thank you to everybody that crossed my path or whose name I didn't mention. I do

this for y'all, so one day hopefully you'll see
His grace, power, and love shining
throughout my words.

El Niño The Prince

This is for you the reader,
I want you to know that no matter how dark
things may seem
You are and will always be the light.
No matter what you go thru
Whether it be heartbreak, loss,
disappointment, or rejection,
Never lose sight of the light that shines
within you and its power to light the way for
another.
No matter how lonely you may feel,
You're never truly alone.
Find the courage to shine that light
And you'll be amazed at the like-minded
souls drawn in by its radiance. We are the
light of the world, never lose sight of that.
Sincerely Yours El Niño the Prince..
When we need it most, God sends a sign.
Some signs are meant to be read, and
that's why we write.
Art Love and Life, A.L.L in between the
lines

Eyeris Morgan

I have met this woman through the rubble
I've picked off the floor of myself after
falling many times in life.
I have sat with her in the mirror, eyes pacing
back and forth trying to genuinely love what
I see.
I have caught her in the palms of my hands
as she ran down my face cupping my
cheeks.
Florencia "Free-Flo" Freeman is a spiritual
warrior. Her words are her weapons as her
wars are her shields. That same warrior
spirit resides in me.
To not have physically met but feel her in
ways I have never felt people I've held or
been held by, is a miracle of love and
understanding only souls can share.
Her writing moves mountains in people, and
the way she weaves her words together as
well as her strength is unmatched in many
ways.
I am truly blessed to be a kindred soul to this
woman in art and life.
Thank you for this opportunity, and for your
bravery in all the transparency you show
through your creations. I Love You, Queen!
#Ase

Tasheka Peterkins

I would like to thank God for blessing me with the talent and ability needed to write this short story. Without Him, nothing would be possible. I would also like to thank Florencia for giving me the opportunity to showcase my talent. Without her, I wouldn't have even considered publishing my story. She has given me inspiration and this platform for which I am extremely grateful.

Thornne Xaiviantt

I would like to first thank Ms. Florencia Freeman for this opportunity in Cutthroat Chronicles. I could not go any further without a much needed thank you to Katrina Gurl, owner of Steamy Trails LLC. I want to thank Cheryl F. Faison for inspiring me to put my writing onto the public stage from the beginning. I also want to extend a thank you to William Peters for the opportunities he has provided me as well. I look forward to producing many more projects in the future and God Bless you all.

Shannon Lang

I would like to thank my mother Alicia M.
Bryant for her continued support
as well as my mentor, Florencia "Free-Flo"
Freeman, for offering me the opportunity to
participate in this anthology with her and so
many other talented authors.
Thank you.

Monroe Borders

I would like to thank all of those who have
pushed me and seen gifts in me before I seen
them in myself
Even though I can't list everyone by name I
would like to thank Shondella A. For loving
me through the good bad and ugly,
Cleveland D. for pushing me and loving me
to the point I found my own strength and
self-love. Thank you. One love

Quiana Golde

First and foremost, thank God for the
inspiration to write and participate in this
anthology. He's guided and kept me for
years and He deserves all the praises I can
give. For Flo to even consider me for this

anthology is a blessing and I want to extend my thanks to her for asking me to be a part of it. I'm so glad my name is on that cover. Look at me!
Thank you to myself for believing in and not deceiving myself. I'm proud of me for me. And with that, enjoy the anthology.

Free-Flo

Thank God for the pain that birthed the desire to write during all those days I spent alone in my room, creating my own world. To my kids, Sylvester Jr., Soraya, and little man that is on the way, Omari. Everything I do is for the 3 of you. To anyone who has ever supported me in any of my business ventures, to all my REAL friends who know the real me and accept me with all of my flaws. To the Team Supreme, Quiana, Tasheka, and Thornne for joining me in this anthology. Thank you for trusting me with this process and riding the waves with me at each hiccups. And finally, to the readers. Without you, there is no us! Enjoy!

A Mother's Love

By: Quiana Golde

A MOTHER'S LOVE

Quiana Golde

Shonda's POV

I woke up with a groan; a long weary groan that seemed to knock the wind out of me. For a moment, I had no clue where I was. Everything was a blur—literally and metaphorically. I couldn't see straight or clearly and my mind along with my thoughts were groggy and fogged.

I didn't have the energy to do anything but blink and try to get my mind right. My body completely failed me, and I was only 26 and in my prime. I never had health issues before so this, was a surprise.

Slowly, my sight cleared up. I was in the dark, but I could make out the fact that I was in the living room of the house I shared with my husband of four years. I could see the kitchen too. Everything was untouched, and it would look like I had been asleep all day. But I couldn't remember anything.

I couldn't remember going to bed last night or waking up the next day. A whole day was gone blank in a blink of an eye.

I felt the panic start to rise and build up inside of me along with confusion. Did I sleep out an entire day?

That meant James came home to absolutely no dinner. Why didn't he wake me earlier then? He would never let me sleep on the couch. Ever. He thought it was bad for my posture and he was right because my neck hurt and so did my lower back.

James... He should be home, but I didn't hear anything. Finding the energy, I turned around and furrowed my brows. Everything seemed normal, but I didn't hear anything.

Looking over to the grandfather clock he inherited from his father, I wrinkled my forehead even more. It was only a little bit after 10. There was no way he would be asleep. Maybe he was in the study poring over cases...

Standing up rather weakly, using the dark brown, leather couch for support, I started on my journey to the study. My legs felt weak and like they were about to give way, but I knew it was mostly because my mind was still foggy.

Sighing, I walked continuously, using the walls for support until my mind came back to normal. "James?" I called out, pushing the study door open. It was empty, untouched.

I was worried... worried and frustrated. But it was a big house... maybe he was taking a shower. Which would be odd considering he came home at 7 and the first thing he did was shower. Even if he stayed at the corporation a little late, he'd still be home by 9 the latest and would've showered already. And the kitchen was untouched too, so I was sure he couldn't be home. Because he loved his food.

Nothing was adding up, not one damn thing. His shoes were at the door, so he was supposed to be home.

Sweeping a hand through my natural tresses, I sighed and started up the stairs to head to our bedroom. I couldn't shake the feeling that something bad happened. It was my instincts. But I hoped I was wrong. I loved James. I couldn't lose him.

The first time I saw him, I was a junior at Harvard University and him a senior. He exuded power and authority and rightfully so. His father was a federal judge... an influential man. So of course, he walked in his father's footsteps.

I knew his last name. But Reid was a popular last name, so I wasn't sure. He came over to talk to me and the rest is history.

We had undeniable chemistry and I just knew he was the one for me. I threw all my plans out the window for him. I wanted to become a lawyer but then all I wanted to be was his woman.

He was old fashioned anyway and believed I was supposed to be in the home so that's where I stayed. People thought that my dad being a senator meant that it was some kind of business relationship, but it wasn't. It was genuine love that I loved.

He was my rock and shield, my source of strength and my literal everything. He looked out for me, made sure all my needs were met and all my wants too. He was the definition of perfection, so I broke my back to make him happy.

To think something was wrong with him was killing me and eating me alive. I found some extra strength and walked even faster towards our bedroom.

"God please let him be home, please let him be okay" I prayed to myself as I wrapped my hands around the cold knob of our bedroom door.

Why was it even closed? We had no reason to close it... it was always fucking open.

With my heart beating out of my chest, I spun the lock and opened the door. I wish I never did. I wish I stayed on that couch and never woke up.

All the energy I couldn't find before built up and came out of me in an ear-splitting scream that hurt my own ears.

James was in the room alright. Spread out across the bed covered in blood. Our silk blue shirts were purple now with the way his red blood mixed with it. The air smelled significantly like iron.

He'd been here for a while because the blood was starting to dry...

It was only his head. His head was split open by a bat. How did I know? The bat was sitting right next to him.

I was hysterical. I couldn't remember a damn thing. I couldn't remember him screaming or crying for help. I couldn't remember a fight. All I knew was, I didn't do it.

I ran over to his body and practically fell on him. I was panting as I shook him. "James, no. Please… you can't be dead…" I mumbled, arms frantically shaking the cold, dead body.

I took up the bat and threw it away from me. I didn't want it anywhere near me. Grabbing his face, I held it in my hands and cried. Just cried.

The love of my life was dead with his eyes open like his head. His blood was all over the room we used to make love in. He was gone, and I had no idea who hurt him. I didn't know who hurt him and why.

Who could? He was so perfect. All he did was go to work, win cases and have sex with me. Work, work, home. That was all. And now he was dead.

I was sobbing uncontrollably. My body shook, my heart hurt, and my throat was dry and tight. I felt like I was going to die. Maybe I should've died right then with him. I didn't want to live without him. He made my bad days good and my good days even better. What would I do without him?

WHO DID THIS?

I had to call the police. I had to call my parents. I had to do something.

Dropping his body back to the bed, I went to find my phone but since I couldn't recall anything, I went to the home line instead.

Picking up the receiver and coating it in blood, I dialled the police. "H-Hello? My husband... I can't remember anything. He was murdered please help" I said, voice as shaky as my hands were. Even my legs were shaking. I couldn't stay still. How could I when my whole world came crashing down?

"Could you tell me where you live ma'am?"

I had to take a moment to gather my thoughts to remember exactly where in fucking Florida I lived. Eventually I remembered that I lived in Naples. "Um, 12 Las Brisas Way, Naples Florida... Please hurry..." I whined like a helpless puppy.

"It's James Reid's residence, this is his wife Shonda Palmer-Reid." I said in hopes of getting them here quicker.

Everyone knew James or at least my father. So maybe they'd treat it as an emergency.

"The police are on their way right away Mrs. Reid" she assured me. I could hear the urgency in her voice, so it must have worked.

I hung up, or tried to, because the phone didn't make it to the receiver. I couldn't stop shaking one bit. I still couldn't believe it. He was dead.

I couldn't bring myself to go back to the room. I didn't want to see the body again. I didn't want to believe it. It wasn't true.

I took up the phone again and made a few calls. One to my parents and one to my best friend Chantelle. They both said they were on their way, but they didn't get here before the police and ambulance.

I said he was dead, he didn't need an ambulance... There was no way to save him anymore, but I guess it was protocol.

They went to the room and before I knew it, the house turned into a crime scene, neighbours came to see what was wrong and I was wrapped up in my parent's arms, shaking and sobbing.

"Baby what happened?" Mom asked me, her doe brown eyes piercing into mine.

I shrugged. "I don't know. I woke up and I can't remember a thing... I can't remember if I even went to bed last night. I knew he was there because his shoes were at the door, so I checked the study, but he wasn't there... then I went up to the room and there he was" I recalled, voice breaking towards the end of my sentence. I couldn't handle this.

I felt daddy's strong hands rub against my back to try and soothe me. "We'll find out what happened baby. The police will do forensics and if anyone was in the house, they'll find out. Did you talk to them already?" he asked me, pulling me towards the car.

I only nodded and looked towards Chantelle who looked sympathetic towards me. "I'll be in the car soon. Just give me a minute" I murmured and walked over to her. I hadn't gotten to talk to her since she came.

"Girl. This is some bullshit. What happened?" she asked in her high-pitched voice that she couldn't keep low. I didn't mind it anymore.

"I don't know Chan. All I know is I woke up and he was dead... I can't remember one thing. I just know I didn't kill him" I said and sighed, rubbing my temples.

"I know you didn't. You can't even kill a baby spider much less the man you loved so much. This don't make no sense... you are going with your parents?" she asked, nodding towards the waiting Cadillac.

I nodded. I couldn't stay in that house anyway. The police were doing all their investigations tonight. They took my phone and already called in the necessary entities to solve the mystery. "I'll call you tomorrow okay?"

"Alright. Try to sleep tonight and remember something baby" she cooed and gave me a tight hug. Her hug was comforting but I couldn't shake the memory of him spread out across that bed with his head split open.

He was his father's only child. I didn't want to imagine how devastated he was going to be once he found out. I didn't have the heart to tell him. I was sure he'd see it on the news very soon.

I went to my parents and they brought me home. Honestly. I really wished I never ever woke up from that sleep. Because the next day was no better.

Chapter 2

Shonda's POV

"You're under arrest for the murder of James Reid."

Of all the things in the world, I never thought I'd be arrested for the murder of the husband I dedicated my entire life to.

It was all over the news already that he was dead, and they were working to find out who did the horrendous crime of killing him. But I never thought in the end, I would be the one getting arrested.

I couldn't even remember shit. But that turned out to be a 'strange convenience' since I seemed to lose my memory when my husband died.

Did I have a reason to kill him? No. But according to pictures sent to my phone from a number I don't even know with my husband apparently cheating on me... that was probable cause. My fingerprints were on his body and the murder weapon and it was the only one in the house other than his.

But it's my fucking house... of course my prints were there. And I touched him.

It was labelled a crime of passion. And I couldn't remember anything because I was so 'angry' and 'hurt'. And because I didn't want to believe it all, my brain just deleted the whole thing. The explanation was backed up by a psychologist, so you know it had to be true.

It wasn't true. There was no way in heaven or hell I could've killed James. Even if he cheated.

Oh, it didn't stop there. I asked how it was me if I woke up clean. They claimed I took a shower. Proven by the blood in the bathroom and bloody clothes there too.

With me not remembering anything, I looked guiltier. So, with no doubt... I went to jail. I'm sorry, not jail. Prison. Prison for third degree murder. Also referred to as a crime of passion. The result... 15 years in prison.

******

Prison was a horrible place. I barely ate, barely slept. I didn't do anything but follow orders and try to stay away from trouble.

I did get the eyes and questions. Was he cheating? How did you do it? Was he gay? Rumours and stipulations that I brushed off while trying not to be rude to anybody. The last thing I wanted to do was piss off somebody in prison.

Every time I saw myself I looked different. I cried too much so my eyes had big puffy bags underneath them. I lost weight, my hair and nails were dry and brittle. I looked and felt lifeless. I didn't feel beautiful anymore… I felt ugly and alone.

My cheeks were deflated, eyes sunk in... my lips were chapped... everything was wrong in my life. Starting with my dead husband...

I was released after 10 years of being in prison. On parole of course and because of 'good behaviour'. I think it had something to do with my dad, but I didn't push it.

My parents picked me up, concerned about my wellbeing but it didn't matter. I was 35 with a bad reputation. With a fucking police record. Me... police record.

And yet I still couldn't remember shit. I couldn't remember anything, and it bugged me. I thought I'd remember

something from dreams of just anything...
but the only thing I could recall was a sound
of clicking heels... clicking heels and
creaking. But that was all. None of those
would help me out.

So, I went back to my house. The
house I shared with my dead husband. Mom
said it was a bad idea, but it was my house
and there was no way I was going to sell it. I
was going to live in it.

Chantelle was waiting on me to
come home with balloons in hand. It was
refreshing to see her after all these years.

"Hey…" I greeted weakly, giving her an equally weak ass hug. I couldn't squeeze her if my life depended on it.

"Let me tell you this, because you know I'm straight up. You didn't kill your husband honey. So, we got to talk. Let's go inside" she said without even greeting me. She didn't ask how I was or anything but to be honest… her saying that meant more to me than anything.

We went inside, and she sat me in the kitchen while she went around, whipping up something for me to eat and drink. I could honestly use it. "So… what's happened since I left?" I asked her, sipping on a cup of ice cold water.

"Well... I've had two babies. Two beautiful boys. One is 9 and the other is 5. But we'll have time to catch up after we figure out who killed your husband. And I won't sleep good at night until I find out who did it" she said, speaking real fast.

She was on a mission. But I already gave up hope with that. I already did the damn time... no use prolonging the pain. "And how do I do that exactly? Chantelle... I already did the time for it. It's no use even thinking about it anymore." I sighed and laid my head on the counter.

"I think you were drugged. Remember my ex Matthew… well he knows everything about drugs and all, so I asked him about the memory loss thing and he said there's one of those date rape drugs that knock you out when you take it. When you wake up, you forget everything that happened that day. So, it's like nothing ever even happened," she explained, and I felt a chill run up my spine. Sounds all too familiar.

"But who drugged me? Was there someone here then?" I asked her, face screwing up like Ice Cube's. It was hard to believe.

"While you were in prison, my ass turned an investigator. How convenient is it that James died a week before the little anniversary party ya'll always keep? Who do you usually plan it with?" she asked me, arms crossing over her chest.

I thought for a moment. She was right... Every year since being married, James and I held a little get together to celebrate our anniversary. I almost forgot about that. "Well me and mom. She likes that kind of thing"

Chantelle rolled her eyes. "Mhm of course she does. And why wasn't she here that day helping you plan the party she likes so much?" she asked me, leading up to a conclusion I didn't like.

"Because she was out shoe shopping…" I answered and shook my head. "Chantelle… chill okay. I don't like where this is going." I said honestly.

She was crossing a big line. I kept hearing her say 'your mother'. My mother had been married for too many years to remember and she had been nothing but supportive of my marriage and my relationship. I loved Chantelle, but this was too much.

James and my mother were mutual friends. That's all.

"Mhm girl, you were in prison for 10 years while I was playing Scooby doo. You think I just came here with no evidence to back me up? I'm telling you babe... your sneaky ass mother had something to do with it. I never liked her, and she never liked me either" she said and tossed her phone at me.

Pictures...

"First of all, the pictures on your phone were fake. I had to get niggas to break in the evidence room to get it, but the pictures were fake as fuck" Chantelle continued on her rant.

But my head was spinning like a gig. This couldn't be right.

I glanced down on her phone and she was right. The evidence was there. There was my mother, fabulous as always entering a hotel. Then a few seconds later came James. Then James leaving... then my mother leaving.

My heart hurt. None of the pictures were of them together... And based on the time stamp... it was during his fucking lunch time. All the hotel visits...

"Mind telling me how you got these pictures?" I asked her, voice shaky and breathing shallow.

"Your dad. He hired somebody to stalk your mother... he just wasn't sure who killed him, but I had to threaten this out of him honestly. Kind of" she hummed and came behind me, massaging my shoulders.

My brows furrowed. "Dad knew!" How could he? Why didn't he tell me? Did he not want the drama? Did he not want to break my heart?

I was frantic. I felt like I was about to have a fucking heart attack. My mother and my husband... My mom and James. This wasn't right... No-

The sound of the door creaking made my head hurt. I turned and in strolled my mother. Then came the clicking of the heels. She always wore heels... always wore heels...

The door... that's what creaked.

"Hey baby" She greeted but stopped dead in her tracks when I looked at her.

My eyes were wide, and Chantelle was just frowning at her. She must have felt like a victim.

"You... You and James? You drugged me, and you killed him? Was it you mom?" I asked her, tears threatening to fall.

"What are you talking about?" she asked me, looking genuinely bewildered. But she couldn't deny it anymore.

I knew for a fact that she was here in this house. Hearing the creak, hearing her heels clicking on the floor. She was here to help me plan the party... James did come home, and she gave me a glass of wine... that's where everything went black. It was her. It had to be.

Shaking my head, I stood up and faced her with a confused glare. "I remember... your heels. You gave me the wine... why did you do it? Why James?" I asked and let the tears threatening to fall come down.

She dropped the bag of groceries and stepped backwards, her face screwing up into something of disgust. "Because I loved him... more than I ever loved anyone else. Including you!" she spat at me. And she looked like she really did mean it. She pulled out a gun seemingly from nowhere and pointed it right at me.

"What the fuck is wrong with you!" Chantelle yelled at her and stood in front of me with her arms wide. "You shoot me, and I swear your dead tomorrow bitch!" she threatened.

But I moved her out of the way. "You might as well shoot me..." I sighed and stood in front of my mother. The woman that raised me since I was born betrayed me for my own husband. She let me do 10 years in prison. She broke my heart. I might as well die.

"No fucking problem" she growled and pulled the trigger. I felt Chantelle push me, but the bullet still hit. It hurt but it wasn't nothing compared to the pain in my heart.

I fell and hit my head on the counter and I was out again.

Chapter 3

Shonda's POV

I woke up surrounded by bright light and silence. It was deafening. I felt confused again. I wasn't sure where I was… and why I was here. I felt helpless.

I looked up and at my body. Hospital gown and tubes stuck inside my arm. I was in the hospital.

Groaning, I laid back and closed my eyes as the memories came flooding back to me.

"You're awake"

I distinctly recalled Chantelle's voice. She was here. Glancing to my left I saw her sitting in a chair close to the bed. "Yeah. Hey… What happened?"

"I beat her ass and called the police. What do you mean what I did? 25 to life bitch" she sighed and came over to me, stroking my face lightly. "I'm so sorry baby"

I sighed and closed my eyes again. My mother betrayed me and framed me because she loved my husband. I guess the saying was true. There was nothing stronger than a mother's love.

Breaking The Bank

By: El Nino The Prince

#BreakingTheBank
Tried to show Ü something real/
I guess you couldn't handle it.
3y3 always keep it 100/
My love's as real as it gets.
I kept it 100/
Went bankrupt off the counterfeit.
Damn I thought you was real/
Everybody plays the fool my nig.
I don't throw shade/
3Y3 shine light.
3y3 see thru you /
on my Nicki shit.
My love was real/
Your's was counterfeit.
3y3 still love you/
From a distance bitch.
When you're ready to keep it real/
Maybe oui can
#SparkTheFlameAgain.
If not/
Fuck it that's life.
#PlotTwistCestLaVie/
I tried ya bish.
I was the man of your dreams/
Those were your words not mine.
How could you sleep on me?
Most fall for the idea/
#Few🃏 can handle the reality.
" All men do is lie".
I told the truth/
And you got mad at me.

3y3 showed Ü what was real/
You chose to live in disbelief.
" you'll never find another like me"
/ I wasn't looking the 1st time B.
I was pursuing personal growth/
You were pursuing me.
I'm in your head /
#ProfessorEx.
My legs broke/
3y3 don't chance a thing.
#SoulOnAttract/
Meet me half way 50/50.
You were more like 80/20
/ I don't like that ratio my G.
You used to reflect me/
Over time you switched up on me.
Real love don't fade/
With time and effort
it gets better B.
Love is a battle field/
I'll fight for you if you fight for me.
Once things become #OneSided/
That's when I take my leave.
I'm like the seasons/
Changing up without switching.
I stayed down from Day1/
You're inconsistent chief.
3y3 invested in you/
You didn't do the same for me.
Trey songz /
it's unfortunate... That you didn't believe in me.
Can't reap what you won't sow/
#YouGetWhatÜGive♻ my G.

An Anthology of Deception

Your actions show
You don't give AF/
Your words
hold no weight wit me.
Is #ÜWithMe or what?
You got me feeling like Drizzy/
#SincerelyYoursElNinõThePrince
Say something baby.
Max Ma on

Swords And Shields

By: Thornne Xaiviantt

An Anthology of Deception

Los Angeles California, a city known for famous sports team accomplishments, a city known for attractions in the present. There is an untold story in which people don't talk about. The media was banned from reporting or investigating and the elderly wrinkle their faces when the youth ask about the events. 1991 sparked a year of turmoil for the city. Rodney King's case sparked an epic riot that rocked not just the city but the nation. Police brutality caught on camera seemed to be the key to ending such brutal events in the minds and hearts of those who remember the events that took place that night and for many weeks to come in the aftermath. The story once buried has now resurfaced. How? Well, I'm about to tell you. My name is Andres Raines. I come from a long line of law enforcement officers, judges, and lawyers in my family despite the vigorous upbringing that followed generations in my family. I was 18 years old graduating from high school. Taking the ACT exam was pointless, because I already made up mind to join the Police department. I asked my father a former military Sergeant in the Armed Forces his opinion. He never

gave me a straight forward answer, because
the last discussion ended in   a debate that to
this day, I believe hurt his feelings. I wasn't
about to apologize because I meant what I
told him. He seemed to have a strong hold
on his stance on the topic of white people
having control of the military and law
enforcement. He often spoke of his issues
and trials in his days in both the Army as
well as the Navy. A career spanning 30
years including time as a Sheriff Deputy
afterward. Little did he know, I was not
about making money like the troubled, drug
driven, alcohol induced thugs that plagued
various neighborhoods in the city. To prove
this to him, I would change everyone's life
the day after my high school graduation. He
never saw my next move coming and when I
tell you it was a big move, I mean very bold.

I walked into the living room to find my two
little sisters Michaela and Serenity laying on
the living room floor watching cartoons on
television. Michaela just three years old and
Serenity was nine years old. I stepped over
their fragile ashy legs making my way over
to my father. He set there in his black ripped

leather chair displaying the mustard stained wife beater and army fatigue pants. He is balding in three separate places on his head. Nappy curled chest hairs protruding over the front edge his wife beater. Stomach half showing and all, he seemed content with his less than presentable look. He is constantly smoking his usual Kool super long 100's puffing cancer clouds in the air as if air pollution was his contribution to the world. "Dad, can I talk to you please?" Gasping and coughing he mumbled under his breath slowly.

"What is it this time boy? I need you to finish cutting my yard today. My knees are giving me hell and you know I can't find my inhaler where is it?" That's right this man smokes constantly complaining about a missing inhaler I've never seen him puff one time. I motioned for him to join me in the dining room. He reluctantly followed behind me.

"Dad we need to discuss my application to the department. I have three weeks until the written test and another month to train for the physical fitness test. Please don't ignore me, this is very important to me." My father stared a hole so deep into my chest I felt as if I had been shot with a twelve gage. He only stared at me like that when he was determined to win the battle between him and I regarding this subject. I let him slide once, but today I was not giving into this act of his anymore. I was determined to break him and today was that day.

"Dad I have already signed the application, so you may as well look it over. I am tired of listening to so many people in this neighborhood complain and talk about how these white politicians are not doing anything. They speak of how we as black people need to make a change. Well I decided instead of sitting in a suit and making false promises of change to my people and the world, I would put that uniform on and become the very change I wanted to see." My father snapped out of his Malt liquor trance and snapped his pupils in an upward motion as if I once again offended him.

"Boy you don't understand a Got damn thang I be telling you do ya? Huh? Huh boy? HUH! ANSWER ME BOY!! DO YOU! THEY DON'T WANT TO SEE NIGGAS WIN IN THEIR WORLD!! He shouted. I broke my damn neck both my arms and one leg for years in two branches of that white man's Army and for what? A stupid ass $600 dollar a month pension a bullshit flag and medical insurance that barely covers your sister's medicines. I FOUGHT I BLED AND I SACRIFICED I DID NOT YOU ME!! You mean to tell me you want to repeat my mistake? MY FAILURE!!! I WILL NOT SUPPORT A REPEAT OF THE PAST I JUST CAN'T, AND I WON'T SO STOP BOTHERING ME WITH THIS BULLSHIT SON!!" SO MANY YEARS I DIVED INTO WARS OF BLOOD, GUTS, SWEAT, TEARS, DEPRESSION, AND MORE!! YOU WOULDN'T SURVIVE A DAMN DAY IN MY DAY BOY AND I WOULD BET EVERY LAST CIGARETTE AND BEER IN THAT FRIDGE ON IT!!" He yelled louder and louder with tears in his eyes. I simply stood up and walked over hugging him.

"I am not doing this to repeat your life dad. I am not doing this to make you look bad. I want my sisters to feel safe walking to the corner store. I want them to go on a date without fear of the next rapist in the news. I want to make sure that I made every effort to make the streets here safe for not just Michaela and Serenity but my kids and their kids too. If I don't do something, the white folks will continue to do nothing and continue to win with each day that passes. I can't sit around and let that happen. That is something I won't do. I hear people say go to college, get an education, and for what? A life time of debt and no progress? C'mon now Dad that is a trap if I ever saw one. They are charging more money to go to school than the jobs those degrees are supposed to get you pay. I can't be a part of that cycle either. I decided that there is more importance in making a difference than to make a lot of money. I hope you will understand that when I graduate the academy and step out on my first day."

My father looked down at me releasing his sagging wrinkled arms from my frame. I can't remember the last time we an affectionate moment, so this was quite awkward for both of us. My father stood five feet nine. In his youth he was a chiseled 190 pounded tattoo machine. Now 48 years old, his once dynamic frame had dwindled down to a storage tank of beer. Tattoos stretched too thin to recognize. Blood shot eyes from nightmare filled nights chasing sleep that seemed to run from him like refugees fearing deportation. His knees shook as he sat back down in his chair.

"Ok son, you win. I only hope you understand what I'm talking about the first time you fire that gun and they are looking at you as if the criminal on the receiving end is the victim. If this is what you are so passionate about then I guess I have no choice. I just want you to have a better chance than your mother," he paused as that last word escaped his mouth. Tears burst from his eyes slamming onto the table piercing the cherry wood stained structure beneath him.

"I just…. I just…."

"What is it dad?"

"I just don't want you to fail your sisters the same way I failed you your sisters and your mother. I quit the department because she begged me to quit but I put the job first. I stayed gone on twelve hour shifts only to get a radio call that I had to go home. Son I walked into my own home to find her shot and killed by some punk teenagers. If I would have taken the day off and stayed home, she would be alive today."

"So, this is about mom and your guilt? Mom didn't die because of you. Mom died because the sons of bitches that broke into our house were cowards who deserve the death penalty as far as I'm concerned. They were heartless thugs and they are still at large to this day. These politicians won't take their ties off and their shiny shoes to catch them. They will sit in their chairs in Washington collecting their ridiculous checks making laws for crimes they were the first to commit. I refuse to sit here and watch this place this environment we all have a right to live in slip between my fingers. That's the bare-naked truth dad and you know it. I am not going out here and destroying the city like those people did in the Riots dad. I am going out here to rebuild the city one person at a time. I may not be able to save the entire world with the years God will give me, but you and my sisters are my world. I believe I can make this world safer for all of you. I want to do my part and I can with your help. My question is, will you help me get ready? Please?" Tears began to fall from my own eyes. My father approached me this time pulling me up from the chair I was sitting in.

"Ok…. ok…I will" My father said this with the softest voice I had ever heard him use in years.

My sisters walked into the dining room wrapping their arms around me crying too. I promised everyone in the room I would give my best effort to fulfill my promise. A promise I started training to prepare for the very next day at 5 o'clock in the morning.

A bright light pierced my pupils as my father stood over my bed waking me up. He told me if I wanted to be the best at the job then I to eat sleep and breathe the job literally. I sat up placing my size fourteen feet on the floor socks dangling hallway off my feet. Stretching my frame to the sounds of popping joints I looked over to see my father picking up the clothes plastered across the floor in my room.

"If you're going to be the best at law enforcement, it starts at home. You can't maintain order in the streets if you can't maintain order at home. I will help you not do it for you. Clean this room up and do it now. Meet me at Victory Park after you have finished the dinner dishes from last night, taken out the trash, mopped the floor, and cut the rest of the grass you did not finish yesterday. Oh, and I suggest you eat light because I will be driving the clunker behind you while you run this mile and a half run too."

Now the sound of chores normally made me Gag and con the girls into doing it for me. I had never been so happy to do chores in my life. My father's support suddenly took a different perspective. He tried his best disguise a half smile on his face, but I know better. My goal to join the police department was indeed his second chance and the long stare of a heated moment turned into a look of commitment and trust. I cleaned my room as instructed then walked into the bathroom down the hall. I stared into the mirror thinking about how much excitement was ahead. I brushed my teeth. My father peeped into the doorway handing me some boxers, t shirt, and socks.

"Hurry up we don't have all day, time won't always be on your side son, time is off the essence let's move and move quickly, get this place in order so we can get started son"

I smiled as I reached for the clothes. "Thanks dad" Now I was ready to take on every training challenge. After my shower, I walked into my room and began to dress myself in a pair old gray mesh shorts and matching gray tennis shoes. I walked into a smoke-filled kitchen with the sun beaming through the window above the sink full of dishes. I placed my headphones on my head and tuned my IPod to the sounds of NWA's smash hit Straight Outta Compton. I Placed the IPod into my right arm brace on my bicep and began the day's cleanup process. Twenty minutes later after finishing the dishes, I mopped the kitchen floor with the smell of Clorox bleach in the air. I wiped all the counter down with the old blue and gray stripped towel as well as cleaning the tomato sauce and ramen noodles Serenity so kindly left behind in the microwave that day. I cleaned the old General Electric stove and oven scrubbing it down with the S.O.S pads and oven cleaner. I called for Michaela.

"MICHELA!! COME HERE PLEASE!" Ten seconds later, she arrived in the kitchen smiles beaming. Michela was my little helper unlike Serenity who thinks every man is to cater to women like queens from the history books.

"Yes?" she said in her quiet squeaky voice

"Come here sit down please" I said just as softly.

"Listen, I know you heard dad and I arguing earlier. I want you to know that things are okay, and nobody is mad anymore okay? I want you and your sister to know that things are going to be different around here. The days of being scared to walk to school? All that is going to be over real soon I promise. I am going to make the streets safer for all of us. You do believe me don't' you?"

Michela scooted her chair out, stood up walking over to me. She gave me the biggest hug. Before I could say anything else she looked at me with such conviction in her tiny little face.

"I know daddy was mad, but I know you will do really good out there. I just hope you don't forget about us is all" I placed my left hand on her head running my hand through her long black micro braids. With a soft voice I responded.

"I won't ever forget about you, dad, your sister and especially mom. I know things have been tough since Mom died and Dad has had it rough raising us alone since she has been gone. I am going to step up and make sure all of us are okay I promise."

"Promise me you will keep the bad people away from us please don't let them hurt our family anymore. Promise me you will come home every day" Michela said with tears in her eyes streaming her soft cheeks.

"Promise" I said softly kissing her on the forehead and hugging her tightly in my arms.

Michela ran back into the living room to join her sister. Serenity did not say much being the quiet one of the three of us. She simply walked over to me hair wrapped in a swinging pony tail, giving me a hug and returning to the floor holding her teddy bear in both arms. I walked through the living room to the front door making my way outside. I walked down the cement steps to the garage. Turning to my right, the garage door was already open. I glanced around inside at all the old yard tools, paint cans, wheel barrel, three half-built vehicle motors and endless oil stains on the floor. I walked over toward the standing Craftsman tool chest grabbing the Red and black colored lawnmower by its black hand spinning it around and pushing it out the garage. I then walked back into the garage grabbing the 5-gallon white paint stained gas can on the floor. "Damn this is heavy" I thought to myself walking back to the lawnmower outside. Bending at the knees, I reached to open the gas cap with my right hand. I then picked up the heavy gas can be pouring the gas inside the mower filling it to the top. I placed the gas cap back on and was ready to tackle the green beast waiting for me in the front of the house. Cutting the grass took about an hour front and back. I was a hot sweaty mess. My father looked through the living room window watching me with a smile on his face. I spent another thirty minutes trying to clean up the garage too. I did what was able to do so then exited the garage walking back up the steps, down a hall, to the living room. I turned right walking back down the hall to my room. I grabbed the bottled water on my cherry oak dresser. I heard my dad walk out the front door telling the girls we would be back soon. I heard another familiar voice immediately.

"Hi Serenity Hi Michela (laughter and giggling) It's me Sha Nae how are you two princesses doing?"

Sha Nae was my next-door neighbor's daughter. She was also the finest black woman you would ever see. Sha Nae was 19 years old, 5 feet 7 inches maybe 130 pounds. She stood there, Light skinned, beautiful brown hair and eyes to match. Staring in the living room dumbfounded inside, I witnessed her hugging both my sisters and I was just in awe. I was digging her so deeply and I wanted her so bad. However, the only thing stopping me was her evil ass boyfriend Terrell. I never checked that fool for treating Sha Nae the way he did, because he had too many ties to gangs as well as guns and I didn't want Sha Nae mad at me for being nosy.

"Hey Dre, what's up?" She beamed that addicting smile at me.

"H-H-H-Hey....Sh-Sh-....Sh-...Sh.....Sha Nae....umm...whatcha doing here?" I was mush around this woman. I actually stuttered! Uggghh!! I couldn't believe it. She made my heart beat a mile a minute and my sister Michela called me out before she could answer.

An Anthology of Deception

"He loves you too pieces. He talks about
you to Dad all the time. He spends every day
making mixtapes in his bedroom with the
door closed. He smiles in the bathroom
mirror acting like you are there with him
singing in the shower HA HA HA HA." I
was blushing beyond repair in this moment.
I was speechless but had no comeback to
spare.

Sha Nae smiled so big you couldn't close
her mouth with a vice if you tried.

"Well…umm…ok….well well…I guess I'm
not the only one who is happy because I get
to watch you two today. (Smiling and
giggling softly) It's okay Dre no need to be
embarrassed or shy your dad called me
while you were in the shower asking me to
watch the girls while you two went out for a
while. He's outside waiting for you in his
car. My sisters were so happy when she said
that. They jumped to their feet screaming
like they had just won a prize or something.

"YAAAAAAAY!!! We like it when you
watch us…..can we play Chutes and
Ladders? Oh…..Oh and can we play Hungry

Hippo too? Huh? Huh? Can we? Can we?"
She smiled hugging them with equal love.

"Yes, we sure can. Now…can you girls
excuse me and your brother for a moment?"
The girls adored her so much all it took was
one request. They walked away down the
hall to their rooms.

"Dre…hey…listen….I umm….I need to talk
to you about something. I didn't want to say
it in front of the girls, but this is important. I
tried your cell phone earlier today but didn't
get an answer. You were probably in the
shower." She giggled covering her mouth
with her left hand. She then took my hand so
softly I almost melted right there on the
floor. We made our way to the black leather
couch. I pushed the girl's toys onto the floor
allowing this gorgeous queen to sit first then
I sat down beside her a blushing mess.

"Dre this is about last night. Terrell and I
had a real bad fight and he hit me again. I
am okay, and it didn't leave a mark but I'm
scared Dre. My brother and Terrell don't get
along and I'm afraid to tell him because I
can't handle any more violent outrages

between those two. I am telling you but please don't tell Mike. He would go ballistic. Promise me you will keep this between us."

I stood up grabbing her soft skinned right hand as she stood with me.

"I got you, I won't say a word. I have to run right now. Listen, we can talk more later tonight is that cool with you?"

"Sure" she said with a small tear welling in her right eye.

"Hey, thanks for watching my sisters too. They really look up to you Sha Nae"

I turned to walk away toward the front door to the sound a horn from outside.

"If only you knew I love you too Dre…so much…" she whispered to herself watching Andre walk out the door.

I walked to find my father playing some old school jazz as usual. He loved his Cutlass too. It was gray, nice rims, a black pin stripe around the bottom, and a little rust around the bumper and some cracked glass on the passenger window and side view mirror. As I made way around to the passenger side, I smiled because he was smiling.

"Well boy you getting in or chickening out? We have business to handle let's go let's go."

I sat down and closed the door to the sound of rusted chants for help from the rusted parts holding the door together, I looked at him with a bigger smile.

"Dad, if you are going to help me train, we can't role to this, I'm sorry."

I removed the disc from the CD player and popped in some real training music. My personal favorite, "Eye of the tiger". My father just laughed, reaching over me opening my door.

"Oh, and by the way who said we?" He then pushes me out onto the pavement then turns up the music backing out the driveway whipping the car around facing toward the long stretch of road aimed toward the subdivision.

"Well, get up, and get those Converse moving son."

I couldn't help but laugh standing to my feet knocking the dust from my shorts. As I walked toward the front of the car, I turned my head around to find both my sisters and Sha Nae peeping through the living room curtains. I cracked a smile waving to them as I started my strides in front of my Dad's clunker.

"Nae Nae what is Dre doing?" Serenity said softly.

Sha Nae stroked her hair with her left hand patting her on the head.

"I don't know, maybe he just wants a little exercise pumpkin"

That was the beginning of some of the most intense training I had done in my life. I received good news just two months into my training for the fitness test. I received my test results from the written exam for the department. I passed with a score of 91 percent. I was only two points behind the top score of 93. I then received a packet in

the mail a couple days later for the fitness
test requirements; a test I would also pass
just forty-five days later. I also passed all the
psychology tests they administered at the
Hall of Justice downtown. These tests were
enough to scare even the toughest of the
tough away but not me. I eventually made
my way to the final stage which was the
Chief Interview. I told my father the good
news when I returned from a picnic with Sha
Nae on a Friday evening.

"Well son, too late to back out now huh?
You really want this bad and I see it your
eyes. You have that there look I had when I
first deployed to Korea as a young soldier.
So, uh…you think you're ready?" He puffed
out a cloud of smoke coughing trying not to
laugh at the same time. I simply smiled at
him because my come back was in my hands
behind my back.

"Well Dad I know I'm ready because these
guys seem to think I'm ready." I handed him
the white envelope in my left hand. Inside
contained letters of recommendation from
four officers were the fathers to a few
friends I had in school as well as letters from

all my teachers all speaking highly of my work ethic and excellent conduct. My father smiled big as that cigarette dangled from the corner of his mouth exposing the three gaps in his yellow stained teeth.

"Well Son, you deserve all of this, you've worked hard. I know I don't say it much, but I am proud of you. I have your back whatever you need. I just want you to succeed where I...."

I reached over quickly covering one side of his mouth carefully avoiding the cigarette side.

"Don't....say it. You succeeded raising us alone and that's good enough for us don't ever forget that" I removed my hand and smiled at him. I could tell he wanted to cry but fought tears to the end.

"Thank you son.....thank you (tears falling down both cheeks.) I love you so much"

My father was kind of enough to lend me a few dollars to get a good suit for the interview. A solid black jacket and pants with the vest and tie to match. Sha Nae ironed my white shirt with creases that were perfect. The moment would arrive on Tuesday March 10, 1994. Andre walked into the room for his interview. The interview was intense and straight forward as expected. What Andre did not know was Sha Nae had made her way to the building waiting patiently outside the doors. Andre made his way out the double doors. Sha Nae stood up from her seated position on the old wooden bench just two feet from the entrance to the room. "Well how did it go Tiger?"

"Tiger? Really?" I smiled.

"Well if you must know I passed and start Academy training in two weeks. The good news is, they pay me during the entire training process." Smiling Sha Nae hugged Andre tight.

"Dre that's wonderful!! Your dad will be proud. I am proud of you too." I returned the sentiments of her hug without hesitation. This was a moment to remember and I couldn't imagine sharing it with anyone else except my mother. I released Sha Nae looking up to the ceiling thanking God for his mercy.

"Momma I know you're watching. I promise to make you proud too. I promise to give my all just as you gave yours being a queen to all of us. I love you Mom" I said as I Sha Nae and I walked down the steps and across bright black and white squared floor toward the exit. My father was standing by the car trying to look cool as usual.

"Well, what's the word son? Are you in or are you out" He said abruptly.

I looked at my feet as the words escaped me slowly.

"Well…the truth is….ummm…" I'm out Dad.

My father stood there stunned in disbelief.

"Well son they don't deserve you anyway" He said with hurt in his eyes.

"OUT OF THIS SUIT AND INTO ACADEMY TRAINING IN TWO WEEKS!! THEY SAID YES DAD!!!

THEY SAID YES!!" I hugged my dad, the two of us spinning around three times laughing and smiling ear to ear.

Sha Nae stood there watching. She positioned a small disposable camera from her pocket into picture taking position snapping two photos of the two embraced in joy.

A year would pass, I had made several arrests in a brief time on my own. The Ride-a- Long phase was over, no more Training Officer heckling from Sergeant Washington, and I was finally in my own Squad Car. I received a call from a private number on cell phone. I waited until I parked the car in the driveway in front of the house to answer. My life was about to change in one phone call.

"Hello…who is this?"

A raspy deep voice answered on the other end.

"Well, well, if it isn't the weather man himself. The fools on the Television station said there was 80 percent chance of turning snitch. What a story what a story. He goes from a homie you can ride and die for on a dime to joining forces with One Time. Captain Save a Hoe! (snickering) so... let me ask you something Rookie, how does it feel?"

"Who is this" I said.

"I'M ASKING THE QUESTIONS HERE NIGGA SHUT THE FUCK UP AND LISTEN!! I hear you're the new hero in town. Running around flashing lights n' all. Feels good doesn't' it? People asking questions, knowing all the right answers, chasing down the bad guys, locking them away, and bringing home a check in the process. Wow, doesn't get any better than that right? Saving the lives of those you love in the city that watched you grow into a man. Well I'm here to tell you this my city motherfucker and you don't run shit I do."

"Who is this dammit" Now I was getting real pissed with him.

"Oh, you may not know who I am, but your old man knows exactly who I am. Why don't you ask him? After all, he has seen my work at its best. Speaking of which, I have someone here who can tell you just how hard I work.

(Voice quivering and sniffing) "Dre it's me Sha Nae he has me and my kids….he wants…"

"SHUT UP BITCH I DIDN'T TELL YOU TO SAY SHIT ELSE SHUT THE FUCK UP!! (Sounds of slapping and crying) Listen real carefully superman. You have twenty minutes to meet my man "T Bone" at the corner store of first and Broadway. Oh…and just you. If I so much as see or hear another cop other than your rookie ass? I'm putting my dick in her mouth to gag her and a bullet in her pretty little head to body bag her you hear me boy? Twenty minutes….be there.

Life began to show me the other side of being a cop quick. Since the riots, crime began to take root growing increasingly more frequent in several areas throughout the Los Angeles area. I had no idea what the hell was going on, but it was now my job to find out. This is not what I was accustomed to watching on television as a child. I quickly ran into the house to change running past both my sisters never saying a word. My father was in the room sleeping two doors down. I quickly changed into some jeans as well as my favorite Gracie Jiu-jitsu T-shirt. After lacing up my black Timberland boots, I quickly loaded my Police issued Glock 25 automatic pistol placing it in the black holster on my brown belt. I loaded three extra 13 round clips into the clip holder also on my belt. I placed a Glock 26 in the small of my back and two clips for it in the front zipper pocket of my black leather jacket. I place badge on my waist just above my front left pocket of my pants. I slid into my leather jacket and black fitted cap rushing out my bedroom door. I ran to my father's room telling I had to go.

"15 minutes and counting" I thought to myself. Time was quickly running out and I had to be across town in a hurry. I was lucky because I convinced my superiors that I deserved a take home car despite the three years wait rule. This wasn't your average take home cop car. A fully loaded turbo charged 5.0 Saleen edition Ford Mustang. Painted department style lights n' all. I jumped in starting the roaring monstrosity under the hood. I blazed down the street with sirens, red and blue lights on the roof flashing to bypass the congested traffic downtown. Within ten minutes with 5 to spare I arrived at my destination. Snatching the keys from the ignition, I quickly hopped out the driver side closing the door and triggering the alarm with my keys. I walked toward the Corner store slowly. (Phone rings)

"Hello?" I said nervously

(Heavy breathing) "Dre…..Dre….please don't let him hurt my babies…please (crying and sniffing) He wants you to go into the store" (Phone disconnects)

"SHA NAE!" I shouted but she was gone. I quickly approached the store and my phone rang again.

As I walked to the entrance, the lights inside flashed on and I could see figures in the back of the store. These weren't your average thugs. They were dressed in police issued uniforms! I recognized one of them right away.

"Terrell?" I said stunned and surprised. "What the hell?" I brandished my Glock out the holster faster than ever.

"Well, well, look who actually made it on time. It's the rookie sensation himself Mr. Gaines how nice of you to punctually join the party sir. I hate to break the news to you but uh…my boss couldn't make it tonight."

"LET HER GO MAN LET HER GO!!" I shouted as I walked toward the four men standing just 20 feet in front of me.

"You can stop right there, Hero or else her brain eats a hollow point for breakfast leaving us all with a bloody Mary to drink if you catch my drift. Drop the gun on floor and kick it over there, Hot- Shot." Terrell pressed the gun firmly to Sha Nae's head. "What? YOU THINK THIS IS A JOKE? NIGGA I SAID DROP THE FUCKING GUN ROOKIE!!"

"Okay...okay...alright...just....don't hurt her please. Here..... I'm dropping the mag and kicking my gun to you relax." Andre kicks to gun away tossing the magazine to the left into a nearby plant setting on the floor.

"Now, now, now, we can finally get down to business the way I like it tonight. You see Rookie, you and I have something in common. This bitch used to be my woman. Well, apparently on the outside anyway. That is until I found out she was yours too. What do I mean? I mean the diary entries I found talking about how she wants to leave me n' shit like that. Saying shit like I dream of another and his name is Dre. The fuck? Really bitch? Really? Well tonight, I and my fellow officers are going to turn her dream man into her worse nightmare. I happen to have an electronic timer strapped to well...."your" girl here hero. Terrell opens Sha Nae's jacket quickly revealing the Syntax explosives duck taped to her body along with a timer. "Oh, and I forgot to mention the five pounds of explosives strapped to her too. This game is called

Black N' the Box. You see I brought four brothers with me. I figure you know what? Word around town says you pretty good with your hands. You know, doing all that Karate, Judo, whatever the hell it is.   Open your jacket let me see your shirt nigga.

Andre slowly removes his jacket placing it over a booth close to him.

That's right GRACIE FUCKING JIU-JITSU!! Well tonight we are going to find out just how good Mr. Gracie is. I'm setting the timer at 8 minutes. You have that amount of time to make it past the four men in front of you! Oh and of course, there is the small task of this bomb turning all ya'll asses into a black charred mess. You stop them, you have a chance to stop the timer, and you stop this bitch from dying. But guess what Rookie? You don't get me sucka.   Yeah, I read in her diary how you want you to whip my ass n' shit too. Well you got to catch me first Rookie. Your time starts now. Terrell clicks the timer and Andre is rushed by the first adversary quickly as Terrell runs out the store through the back door down the dark hallway. It was literally do or die time.

The first assailant 6''2 240lb dove for Andre's legs. His long arms reached frantically however Andre quickly sprawled backward, stuffed the takedown, wrapping his opponent's neck with his left arm, and his own wrist with the right hand. Bringing himself to a rapid-fire speed standing position choking the man for a few seconds, Andre quickly releases his wrist spinning around turning his back to his foe with his arm still wrapped around the neck of his enemy. Pulling down hard and quick with one arm snapping the neck instantly killing the attacker. Dropping the body to the floor with Seven minutes thirty-two seconds left, he waved his next adversary to him with his right hand.

The man stood 5''8, short corn rolled hair and 190lbs. Light skinned, and stocky. He brandished a baton from his belt swinging and twirling it fast racing toward Andre shouting "YOU'RE GOING TO DIE TONIGHT!!" Swinging the bat on with his right hand toward Andre's head, there was

no time to waste. Andre pulled his back up
Glock quickly shooting the man knocking
him to the floor with three center mass shots
to the chest. Andre then pulled the trigger
five more times putting another bullet this
foe's head and two bullets in each of the
next two enemies who rushed in. As the
time reached 5 minutes forty-five seconds,
the side door entrance bursts open, hinges
and wood crashing to the floor. Andre stood
there stunned not expecting additional
confrontation. The Goliath monster in front
of him stood 6 feet 8 inches 350 pounds of
solid rock muscle mass. Removing his black
leather best quickly flexing. His bald head
dripped sweat down to glazed rage filled
eyes of pure terror. The monster of a man
grabs Andre by the neck with one large hand
lifting him right straight in the air despite the
three jabs to the sternum. One choke slam to
the floor later, Andre was gasping air which
was quickly knocked out of him! He laid
there for a few quick seconds before his
blurred vision was blocked by the blurred
mass of the beast above his motionless body.
Grabbing both of Andre's legs in each hand,
the giant swung Andre around in a circle

twice launching him into shelving knocking over several food items collapsing the shelves in the process. Standing to his feet slowly, Andre removed the blood from the corner of his mouth. "Okay you really want to do this? Let's get it over with" Reaching behind him, Andre removed the Glock 36 from his waist back tossing it to his left side. After removing his jacket, tossing it in the same direction, Andre took a stern fighting stance, motioning for his adversary to approach. Obliging him, the monster lunged forward only to be met with a swift front jump kick from Andre's left boot. Quickly snapping two left jabs and an uppercut to the square hard jaw of his opponent, the beast never moved an inch. He brushed off his chest with his left hand and continued forward. "What the hell is this mother fucker on?" Lunging forward, his opponent dove for his Andre's legs tackling him to the hard floor. Andre quickly wrapped both legs around the behemoth sinching a guillotine choke deep, but the monster pushed out before the pressure could be applied. Once postured up, he launched punches down to Andre which were smothered by the sharp punch block series defense he had perfected in his early training days. Pushing the left arm north, Andre managed to sneak his right leg through the gap setting himself up into a triangle set up position. Pushing the right arm of his foe over across his waist, Andre raised his hips locking his left leg over his right angle sinching a tight Triangle choke. Six crucial seconds later, the giant went limp no longer resisting. Releasing the hold, and pushing the man to the side, Andre stood on his feet to see 2 minutes left on the timer and frantic look of terror on ShaNae's face. "PLEASE GET ME OUT OF THIS THING" she screamed. Andre found the timer control just a few inches from her feet dropped by Terrell. "Shit its busted I can't stop it. It's not motion activated I'll have to cut you out!" Removing a small knife from his pocket, He walked to ShaNae with her quivering eyes and lips shaking in terror. "It's okay, I got you. Slowly guiding the knife down the center of the bomb vest and duct tape, he was careful, because one slip of the hand and cutting a wire would set the Syntex off. Ten seconds later with a minute and thirty seconds to go ShaNae and Andre sprint out the side door to his car. "GET IN!" Starting the car, Andre shifts into first, then second, third, and finally fourth and fifth gear speeding desperately down the closest one-way street. "If I can make it to the river, I can toss this thing. "Oh god Dre hurry we are down to a minute" she said frantically. The speedometer jumped to 120 mph lights flashing and siren blazing. Leaning out the window Andre screamed for pedestrians to move out the way. "MOVE! GET OUT THE WAY!" Leaning back in, he lifts to middle console brandishing four small NOS tanks with green lights illuminating. "Hold on this is gonna get real intense boo" Turning four switches and slamming the console shut, Andre pushed two red buttons on the steering wheel launching the car to the 240 mile an hour mark fire bursting from the exhaust pipes. "Okay we are just a few feet from the river, you are going to have to jump out into the brush!" "WHAT! IM NOT...." Andre moved to his right, slowing down just enough to a safer speed. Quickly reaching across her unbuckling her seat belt. NO TIME TO ARGUE!" JUMP NOW!" Sha'Nae opened the door jumping into the brush of bushes. The car speeds off down the street quickly reaching the 140-mph mark. Andre pushes the second button igniting the NOS again racing toward the river just a quarter mile from the spot Sha'Nae jumped. Rolling a couple times, she quickly raises up to watch the Mustang blaze down the street. "Lord please let him make it" she said to herself. "twenty seconds to spare gotta go now" Andre pulls the E brake turning the wheel sharply the left sending the car into a perfectly executed drift slide toward the riverfront's edge. Lowering the driver side window, he tossed the bomb vest into the river. Immediately speeding off, within another ten seconds, water erupts from behind. Stopping sharply, he reached Sha'Nae and she races to the passenger side of the car. "What the hell is going on?" She said abruptly. "I do know but your pissed off boyfriend seems to be involved with some shady cops, something I didn't have any idea about. I also did not know the department I just joined is now being disbanded. Something doesn't add up. All I know is, your boy tried to kill you and me for a reason and I am willing to bet I can find him and the truth in the same place." "What are you going to do?" Andre....what are you going to do?" "I don't know but there is definitely handcuffs, jail and one hell of an ass kicking in Terrell's future."

After fifteen minutes of driving, Andre pulled up to his Dad's house. Jumping out quickly he races to the front door to find a note. "IF YOU LIVED TO READ THIS THEN MEET ME AT THIS ADDRESS. OH AND YOUR DAD AND SISTERS SAID HELLO ASSHOLE" "SON OF BITCH HAS MY FATHER AND SISTERS" FUUUUUCK!" Running frantically back to the car, Andre snaps his seat belt back in, shifting into reverse, the mustang screeches backward spinning to a forward position. Launching from zero to sixty in 5.7 seconds, Andre was beyond angry. "Something is wrong, what is it Dre?" "Son of bitch has my father and sisters". He hands her the note from the door. Pounding his left fist into the steering wheel's edge. "You're going after him alone? He has to have friends in on this" "Exactly"

Andre said. "I'm calling in a little insurance policy" Andre radios for backup to the address on the note. "Officer Raines badge #4572 off duty. I have a hostage situation in progress. I need the Swat bus and all available units to 35th and Bank street immediately over. " The dispatcher responds but it's not the response he expected. "I told you young buck I own every inch of this city. They may have disbanded our unit, took food out our families' mouths, but Im taking this city back tonight. If you don't hurry Im killing the man responsible along with these two sniveling runts too." Radio signal dies. "Shit, that asshole is crazy."

"Andre, I swear he never told me he was involved with any of this I never knew I swear I didn't."

Sha'Nae grabbed his hand softly squeezing it. "I believe you but he wanted you dead for a reason, and I'm going to find out why one way or another. If that means killing his ass then so be it."

Ten minutes later, they pull up the address. There is a dense fog covering the area.

"I don't like this shit stay in the car and lock the door. Open the glove box and hand me my .45"

Sha'Nae hands him the gun with shaking hands.

"Dre please be careful." She leans in as he turns to face her. Kissing him slowly and softly on the lips. He caresses the side of her face before exiting the car.

"I will be back with my family. I don't want you in harm's way again. Not again, not after what we just went through. If you want to help me, stay here. There is an extra cell phone in the console try to get back up here. I have contacts from a neighboring agency. Get help here. I know he won't be alone. He's too smart for that." Andre exits the car walking into the abandoned building with ambers flying all over the place.

"Looks like an old factory building with some activity still going" he thought to himself. Andre loaded a 13-round clip into the GLOCK .45 caliber handgun raising it slightly keeping an eye out for anything suspicious. After walking and turning several corners cautiously......a voice booms from behind him. "ANDRE GET OUT ITS A TRAP SON!"

"DAD?" Turning around to his right, he sees Terrell holding a silver-plated Smith N' Wesson 9-millimeter handgun to his father's head. Two goons roll both his sisters out duct taped to office chairs with their mouths duct taped too.

"I told you this city belongs to me boy. You thought putting that badge on would fix this city? This world? No, it made it worse. You see, I was just like you. I signed on too. But this son of a bitch you call a father fucked it all up for me long before I got on to anybody's police force. You see, he was supposed to save her. He fucked up and got her killed.

"Her who?" What the hell Terrell? What in the hell are you talking about? You tried to kill Sha'Nae you sent dirty cops to kill me not mention incredible hulk. What the fuck man?"

"I told you I would ask the questions so let's ask your Pops. Let's ask Pops what really happened that day. Let's ask Pops why he really didn't want you to join the force. Why he lied like the sack of sorry shit he really is."

Terrell rips the duct tape from his hostage's mouth.

"GO ahead you lying son of a bitch and tell him the truth!"

"Dre...I... I raped and killed your mother. Terrell is your brother. You were born shortly after and to cover my tracks I hired some kids to stage a break in. I only told them to rough her up. I did not know they would kill her. I staged it to look like I walked into a break in with a struggle. I shot her when she told me she had proof of the rape. I couldn't risk my career. Terrel was born before you. I kept that a secret too I'm sorry."

"What? What the hell is he talking about?" Andre lowers his weapon.

"That's right hero. This sack of shit right here raped my mother which is how your punk ass got here. This bitch hid from me for years. That is until I found him through files I stumbled on at work two years after joining the force. He raped my mother because she was a councilman who voted to disband the very unit that you joined years later.

Andre stood in disbelief. He couldn't imagine what he was hearing much less hear it.

"Yeah, let that sink in rookie. I bet you still think I'm the bad guy here? I wanted you dead because every breath you breathe is a reminder of the lies this piece of shit father of mine told. Your face is a constant reminder of the hell he put me through. Not only that but my bitch leaves me for the man born from a violent crime of hate and deceit. Oh, hell no I wasn't having that shit man!"

The father speaks with a raspy injury filled voice.

"Dre....I'm so...so sorry. I didn't want you to join because you would have found out the truth and I needed you to protect your sisters. I didn't want you to...."

Dre interrupts abruptly

"SHUT UP! I DON'T WANNA HEAR THIS SHIT! HOW COULD YOU DO THIS? YOU LIED!!! YOU MADE UP ALL THESE DAMN STORIES AND EXCUSES ABOUT HOW YOU SACRIFICED. A-L-L-L-L THESE REASONS WHY YOU DIDN'T WANT ME TO BE LIKE YOU!! THE WHITE MAN'S ARMY THIS AND THAT!! WELL GUESS THE FUCK WHAT BOTH OF YOU ARE GOING DOWN.

Andre snaps his weapon forward firing three quick shots. These were two center mass shots to both goons behind the office chairs and one to Terrell knocking him back as his gun is dropped to the floor. Quickly pouncing on top of Terrell Andre rained down blow after blow with his weapon spewing Terell's blood all over the concrete floor.

On his knees in pain, the father of both men pleads for Andre to stop.

"DRE!! PLEASE HE'S YOUR BROTHER DAMMIT!! You kill him...you're.... (breathing heavily) …. you're no better than me. Please don't make the same mistakes I made. Let him go Dre....Let him go son"

Andre raised up for one final blow. Then, as he turned to the man now known as his mother's rapist, he paused.

"You're right I'm not like you."

Andre stands to his feet Pulling Terrell's battered frame with him. He pushes Terrell to an old rusted metal table forcing him to face forward with his back to him.

"You too you're both under arrest."

With his gun still raised, Dre motions for the man who he used to call a father to the table.

"Get over there...."

His father pleads for mercy.

"Dre-Dre- Dre-Dre...I...I..."

Just then a louder female voice from behind the three of them shouted.

"YOU HEARD HIM YOU SON OF BITCH GET OVER THERE WITH YOUR HANDS BEHIND YOUR BACK COWARD!"

Sha'Nae arrived with six other armed officers.

Andre turned in shock as the officers quickly raced over to apprehend the two men.

"Hello son, my name is Lt. Masters. Your lady friend here managed to get an outside frequency that wasn't rigged by this ass wipe. This is how we were able to pinpoint the location and get here in time. It feels good to know there are still some good cops in all this mess. I did know if I had a job either to be honest. The disband of the precinct had us all angry but not enough to stoop to his level of anarchy. Listen, with this bust, this may convince the council along with everyone's testimony to reinstate the entire department. Son you and your lady friend here jus saved lives and jobs as far as I'm concerned, you're a detective from this day forward. These "Swords" are all rebels angry at the disbanding of the force. They turned to breaking the law they swore to uphold. This is not the answer. I'm glad we still had a good shield in all this mess. Who knew a rookie would save the city?

Sha'Nae walks over to Andre hugging him tightly. Andre returned the hug instantly. Kissing him gently on the neck and then slowly on the lips.

"I love you Andre Gaines. Oh, and I have a surprise for you. Your last name isn't Gaines Its Rhaines"

Sha'Nae points toward the entrance and shadow appears in the doorway. As the figure walks closer, another female voice darts from the shadows. Dressed in a black leather jacket black tank top, blue jeans, white tennis shoes, a badge on the belt, and Glock 25 pistol on her hip, Andre received the next shock of his life.

"Hello Big brother, so this is where you have been hiding? I have been looking for you. The name is Jhianna Rhaines......your sister. (to be continued) ....

An Anthology of Deception

Untitled

By: Monroe Borders

The eternal clock was constantly going off without the option to hit snooze. As a five-year-old that only meant one thing. It's Saturday.. time to go play. But something was different about this Saturday it didn't seem the same, mommy was arguing in the living room with what you would call her Main.

The precious 5-year-old called him Mr. Him And Mommy called him bae but after what she seen all he called her was a bitch that day she was screaming and crying and bloody with tears screaming "I want to get my baby out of here."

Because all she kept seeing was him punching kicking and slamming her face and when this five year old couldn't take it she jumped on him without thinking twice he slammed her against the wall to get her off like a little bug and when her mother saw she was crying she screamed "run my love" she ran down the stairs to her babysitters on the first floor hearing her mother scream and get beat even more she couldn't recognize her by the time she came to get her.

the mean man had left but not after putting his hands on her.

they went to the child sister's place where they couldn't even recognize her at the door everybody was crying, and a little girl just kept saying my body is sore.

for more ways than one this man had broken her mother, the person she looked up to and admired.

He broke her, but her mother still had left her there with her sister. She went back to that mean man she said, "I understand him better than anyone can."

Mr. Calvin J Smith is what his name was and who she chose over her daughter that day when she said she was a miracle baby the streets had something else to say.

As time pressed on things started to go on as normal but something still lingered in the girls spirit she couldn't shake quite well.

How could a mother choose a man over her? How could you convince her that she was loved? How could your actions be so treacherous and deceptive?

How could she?

The ultimate hurt was through it all she loved her mother as if she did nothing wrong.

SOS-Saving One's Self

By: Eyeris Morgan

An Anthology of Deception

First person story on becoming an object of self-deception for emotionally closed people.

I wish I hadn't been taught to swim,

Too much seduction to dive in emotional oceans.

Holding my breath on many occasions,

Waiting on people who were more rigid than the seasons.

It seemed as if my body was some kind of catalyst,

But my production of love never made the list.

My smile for many was a natural curve,

Only God could see its hidden dangers.

If it had a mirror it would be climate change,

Only he knew its mood changed every day.

I think the reason our lips curl at the end,

Is to act as barrier for what lies behind them.

I have always been opinionated.

Cutthroat Chronicles

Sometimes when I spoke, men felt
emasculated.

It was never to downplay the size of their
minds,

But an invitation to what lied in mine.

I have had men, who entered me,

Only a few have been inside.

I was the library you went to as a child,

The book you put back once the internet
became popular.

I was the dish you could eat every day,

But takeout made me a burden to create.

I was the song your mother used to sing,

But cassettes and CD's have become
outdated.

I am not a paid advertisement,

You might not find me on the first page.

An Anthology of Deception

A butterfly that scares most from the design
of her wings,

I am the bird they caged because I could
sing.

I am the bones that move behind doors,

And the knob that keeps them there.

I am the product that costs more,

So instead they just cut their hair.

I am the investment most thought was a
flake,

Because I didn't require money: only faith.

The coins people find on the floor,

I add up as time passes.

But no one counts their coins anymore,

And ripped bills end up in the trash.

In order to grow, something has to break.

Cutthroat Chronicles

I placed my repair in the hands of everyone
but me.

Foolishly gripping fragments of glass,

Ignoring how deep they were cutting me.

Eventually self-perception became a scar,

I couldn't let anyone touch me.

What if they pressed too hard?

Then they would break me.

If I let them do that,

They would say they made me.

But what if!

What if I met them, so I could discover me?

I cannot mess up this opportunity.
I'll do everything they ask,

And be whoever they need.

But, would they still love me?

*Would they see my adaptability as part of
who I am?*

Would they understand that we are all the same woman?

If I make these sacrifices, what will be left of me?

If I don't, how will they know the love that is within me?

I thought love was supposed to be easy,

Why do I feel so conflicted?

How do I know this is the right decision?

Is there such a thing as correction when all is fair in love and provision?

I know I stand for more, than doubted miracles and romance classics.

Human centipede: their heads are so far up their asses.

I am nothing short of elemental,

Intimidation was common because I'm essential.

A dimension of wisdoms and perspectives that would crush the hardest ego,

I now see how cavemen came to be.

Fearful of conflicts and endings,

I soothed their lust when it was my value
that needed mending.

Because I was tired of giving my love to
myself,

And I had already felt too independent.

I started to wonder how it felt to be the
"wanted "girl,

It gets old being the one men hate to need.

For once I wanted nothing but to be desired,

The trick a man couldn't wait to pull from
under his sleeve.

But after many heartbreaks and breakdowns,

I learned that role wasn't for me.

I was the woman in a girl's body,

A wife before I knew what marriage was.

The kryptonite to a man's logic,

An Anthology of Deception

I am Love.
 Now I see why people chose me to hide.

But how long can you avoid something that
lies inside?

What Is Deception?

By: Hebrew King

An Anthology of Deception

What's deception? Could it be individuals brainwashing the minority of the poverty-stricken people to follow their religion... I'm not accepted for the art of deception passes my reflection because ass kissing doesn't match my   irrelevance #Kingdomguided... I wondered what's my purpose? Could it be to play sports or direct the lost back to my heavenly father... I'm far from being bothered by the rumors and gossip that never been a problem... I rather follow the truth then follow the coon rules of the NFL and NBA, love me for bringing you championships but can't respect me kneeling to show my gratitude for those killed for being the pigment of ME #weshallOVERCOME... The devil controls it, I'm giving you an ultimatum to follow HIS will or continue to let your brain become corrosive ish is getting REAL... I gotta make it, even if it causes me to venture off of the radar and live off of the land rather than being forced to use the CHIP to buy food and have money again #Back2daBASICS... FATHER, give me the health and strength to follow you WILL and prophesy to the world through my words before I'm jailed or killed #fulfilledDESTINY...

Bed of Lies

By: Tasheka Peterkins

An Anthology of Deception

Chapter 1 Anias 2 months ago

"Anias I'm telling you something has to give! I just can't do this anymore, it's like every time we try to make this shit work it backfires in our faces! .....I think it's time we just admit that things aren't the same"

I sighed as I looked at my wife, she was so beautiful, everything a man could ever want in a woman. Soft curvy features, rich chocolate skin tone, big pretty eyes and the softest lips. She usually covers her lips with a deep red lipstick, however today they glistened with a simple touch of pale pink lip gloss. She wore only a black sheer underwear and a sports bra to match. My thoughts should have been on helping her out of the few garments she had on, but instead I had to pretend to be listening to her as she went on again about our ailing marriage. Let her tell it, our marriage had run its course a long time ago, but I didn't see it quite the same way. Last night, I tried to take her out to her favorite restaurant. I figured if I could just take her back to the times when our love was strong, when it was new and fresh and full of hope and potential, then we could somehow rekindle that and continue from there. However, that wasn't exactly in the plan for us. It started off great. She looked amazing in her sheer black floor length dress the back cut out to show more skin than I would have liked, but, I decided to let it go, if only for one night. I was equally dapper in my tailor-made suit, cut to fit just right. With the naked eye, one would pass us off as the perfect couple, the moment we sat down at the restaurant however, to onlookers it would have been obvious that something was wrong. I tried to tell myself to give her some time, we had just had some big argument a couple days prior and she might still be feeling a little sour from it. To make it work, I made it my point to try to keep a positive conversation flowing, make her smile, be the perfect gentleman and do everything just right. Even with my greatest efforts though, it still felt like pulling teeth with Nyla. It was obvious she didn't want to be there, and I was only wasting my time. I refused to give up though, so I continued with my fruitless efforts until my annoyance overcame me and I found myself calling her out on her pissy attitude. It's not hard to guess that we left that restaurant being more at odds than we were when we went in. We slept in separate rooms that night, as we seem to do most nights these past couple of months. Now this morning instead of awaking to a breakfast made with love I was greeted with an empty coffee pot and a wife who seemed so desperately to want to divorce me. I didn't feel the need to respond to her words because I knew like she did that we would not be getting divorced. There was no out for us. We took that vow before both man and god and if I had any say in it , it will most definitely be until death do us part!

"Nyla, let's not talk about this right now, I have an appointment in a few hours that I can't be late to. I guess it's safe to say that I won't be eating breakfast here thing morning" I said while eyeing the empty kitchen.

"Anias, I know what you are trying to do, and it just won't work! I'm not happy Anias! And I want -"

I didn't allow her to finish that sentence before the back of my hand connected with the side of her face. It isn't often when I hit my wife, however Nyla has a way with words that will make a man forget his upbringing and lay hands on her!

" How! How can you say you are not happy! I work hard just so you can have everything you need! There are no limits in your debit cards! You drive the latest car and live in a mini mansion! All for free! Nyla you are a kept woman! A finely kept one at that, you want for nothing and still....still you complain! Do you know how many women out there would gladly give their souls just to walk a mile in your red bottoms!"

"And what good does it do Anias! What does it profit a man to gain the world, but to lose his soul? You have my soul Anias! You have it, and I want it back!"

"Nyla, I have grown weary of this entire encounter. I'm leaving, you are free to do as you please with the day, but when I return, I intend to be greeted at the door by a loving wife, and wear something sexier than what you have on now, I think it's time you resume your wifely duties" I ignored the look of loathing she held on her face as I made my way towards the door. What my wife knows but fails to accept is that I do indeed have her soul, and I have no intentions on giving it back.

Chapter 2 Nylana

"I don't know what else to do mason. He refuses to listen to reason, he just doesn't care." I put my head down into the palm of my hands as I cried again for the third time since I woke up this morning. I was a shell of my former self. A tainted woman whom if it had not been for a strong will to survive would have succumbed to the many adversities I faced since the very first day I entered this world as a premature five lb.

baby, with a strong addiction to Percocet and oxycodone. My mother was a pill addict and a heavy drinker, thankfully my kidneys were fine, underdeveloped, but fine. I never knew my mother, I grew up in an orphanage. No one wanted to adopt a baby that was already a burden at birth. I was almost destined to be a failure. Bouncing about from one place to the next I refused to allow my circumstances to determine my outcome, so I did as much as I could with as little as I had, graduated high school, and then went to a community college to get my license and certificate as a pharmacy tech. My very first job turned out to be the last, and ultimately the biggest regret of my life.

"Nyla, man there has to be a way for you to get out if this baby! I'm tired of having to meet you in hotels and share you with another man!"

"Well I'm trying mason! But what do you want me to do!"

"It shouldn't be so hard to get a divorce! You can file for one and then petition for a court ordered automatic divorce if he chooses to be stubborn. If he doesn't sign those papers in 30 days then that's an automatic divorce, and if he does, all you have to do is tell the judge about his physical and emotional abuse this will all be over in a short couple of months! We could've already been starting our life together Nyla! Or don't you want that!"

"Don't be ridiculous Mason of course that's what I want-"

"Then why don't you do it!"

"Mason stop! I told you it's not that easy!"

"What does he have that's keeping you from doing this? What's got you so shook baby! Come on talk to me, you know that I love you, and all I want is for us to be together. Please don't shut me out man, let me help you....let me help us!"

"I'm so sorry Mason, I really do love you, with all of my heart baby, but you can't help with this, this is between me and Anias, but I promise you, we will be together soon baby" I responded with a smile while I kissed his lips for good measure. It isn't that I don't trust or love Mason, it's just that after what I'm going through with Anias now, I'd be damned if I put myself in such a situation again. I have to find a way to get away from Anias, once he finds out what I've been doing to pass the days he is sure to make an attempt on my life. With no family and no friends, I find that I have to catch myself from sinking deeply into a bottomless pit of despair. For three years I have been married to Anias, and the first year or so I think we were still in the honeymoon stage, hell we should have still been in it now! But for the last couple of years I have not been happy with Anias. I think a part of me knew from the beginning that I didn't love Anias, well at least not enough to marry him. When he proposed however, and I thought about my life and what I had in it, I jumped at the thought of having a family of my own to love and cherish. For a lot of neglected children, it is hard to consider being a parent to anyone, simply because they don't truly know what the meaning of being a parent is, because they never had one, or the ones they had were awful they automatically assume they'd be the same. Not me though, I always knew I had enough love for a big family and couldn't wait to have one. Now three years later, Anias and I are no closer to starting that family than we were prior to meeting each other or getting married. At first Anias said we weren't ready to start a family and I was heartbroken. But now I'm grateful we hadn't. Anias had brought up the conversation of children some time ago and just like him I said we weren't ready. And continued taking the pills despite him asking me to stop.

"Nyla!"

"Yes, I'm sorry I zoned out, did you say something?"

Mason breathed down heavily before pointing at my ringing phone. I picked it up and hit the ignore button when I saw Anias' name pop up on the home screen. I was in no mood to deal with him now. I was with a man that I loved and that loved me back, so fuck Anias. I turned the ringer off on my phone and placed it at the hotel coffee table as I slowly rose from my chair and seductively began sliding my dress over my thighs. I stopped as I got to the point the color of my panties, which were red, were visible and looked over at Mason and caught the huge bulge on full display trying to burst through his jeans. It was always so easy to arouse both the men in my life, although I have long since stopped trying to be any kind of sexy for Anias. I continued the journey with my dress, until it was all the way off my body. Putting on my finest cat walk I made my way over to Mason whom had already taken it upon himself to start undressing as well. By the time I made it over to him I only wore my underwear, I didn't take it off because I knew how much he loved to. Mason was also only wearing his Hanes boxers. I stood before him playing with my nipples while squeezing my well-endowed breasts. Mason reached out and groped between my legs getting my panties soaked before he left the chair and got down on his knees before me and began devouring my pussy still trapped in the fabric of my Victoria's secrets. Anias would just die if he saw what was happening to the panties he bought but never got a chance to see me wear. Mason eased my panties down to my ankles and I stepped out of them as he continued his assault on my body, in a way that Anias had never done, that nigga didn't even eat pussy! But demanded his dick be sucked every time we had sex. Yea he's a selfish motherfucker! Lost in my thoughts and the feelings overcoming me I gasped as Mason suddenly rose from his knees, lifting me in the process and setting me down across the chair he had just vacated.

"Assume the position!" He demanded, and I wasted no time getting on my hands and knees excitedly anticipating the feel of his 9-inch-long dick inside my body. Mason was only the third man I had been with, before Anias I was dating a guy my age named Jason we were both 21, but Jason was still a teenager at heart and it just didn't work out for us. There are times I wish I had stuck with Jason even though not much has changed with him I still feel as if anyone would be better than Anias. Mason had Anias and Jason both beat by at least three inches and he fit me just right! I gasped and squealed when he inserted the head and then took it back out. "Muthafucker always playing games! Nigga put the shit back in!"

"I just love it when the hood comes out of you during sex. And not that bougie white girl pronunciation and shit"

"Man, just shut the fuck up and fuck me Mason!"

"How you want it?" He asked still teasing the fuck out of me, I almost hoped he would bust while he's there showing off and shit so I could laugh at his dumb ass!

"Mason!"

"Nah tell me how you want it Nylana!"

"Oooo I want it hard Mason! Just give it to me hard and fast!" I screamed from my sexual frustration. Anias and I don't have sex often, however Mason and are be getting it in! I mean what else would we do throughout the day? Anias didn't want me working and Mason didn't really have to. He wasn't filthy rich, but from his small construction company his bar, and not to mention the generous life insurance payment he got from his wife's death by accidental overdose he was sitting pretty. I moaned and screamed as I took everything that Mason had to offer. He was fucking me so crazy, I had come twice already, once from his little teasing session. My mind fleetingly ran across Anias and what he might be doing but quickly changed course as another orgasm left me drained and utterly satisfied.

Chapter 3 Anias

"I just don't know, something about her seems off. I'm starting to believe that she's cheating one me" I was nursing my 6th maybe 7th drink in the last two or so hours at a bar I usually frequented. It's been two weeks since that argument between me and

Nyla and we have barely spoken a word since then to each other. That night I went home and demanded some affection from my wife, but all I got was a lackluster performance if it can even be called that and a bruised ego. I had always prided myself on at least being able to satisfy my wife sexually and arouse her even when she didn't want to be bothered. However, that night due to the apparent disinterest of my wife I had to use baby oil to aid in the process. I wasn't going to stop though. Before then it had been months since Nyla and I had had any type of intimacy with just barely any physical closeness. That among other things have led me to believe that Nyla must have someone doing for her what she no longer wants me to do. If it's one thing about my wife she's no prude, she loves sex just as much as the next guy!

"Come on now Anias, why would you think something like that? Nyla may be mad at you, but I don't think she would ever cheat!"

"Ha, she's more than just mad my friend, she's livid!"

"Well it seems to be bigger than I thought. You too going through something?"

I gave my longtime friend a sideways glance and went back to sipping from my almost empty beer bottle. The fuck was he even thinking? He knows I don't talk about my relationship. Not even to him! Doing that only gives another man, reason and means to get into your relationship.

"Alright, alright, I forgot you don't talk about your relationship like that. But still, I think you're overreacting. Just take her out to dinner and wine and dine her, females love shit like that"

" I tried, she made a huge fuss the entire time and we ended up arguing before we even started our dinner!"

"Wow!" Was all he said.

"So, what you gonna do?"

"I don't know yet. I'm going to have to figure it out though. Nyla knows better than to fuck with me, but she's hard headed just like all these other bitches! Imagine having to use oil on your wife cuz her pussy won't get wet for you!" I was speaking a little too loudly even for my own ears and divulging to my friend way more than I intended to. But that's what alcohol will do to you, change you into a whole other person.

"Come on man, I think we've had enough of the liquor for today, besides I'm ready to call it a night." Usually I would get mad whenever someone tried to regulate my drinking, however I decided to agree to his point and call it a night. I was also eager to go home and confront Nyla about my suspicions, better yet, maybe I won't, if she really is cheating, she isn't dumb enough to admit to it. With my contacts I can hire someone to follow her for me for a while, just to see what she's been up to, I've always been a private person, never letting my left hand know what the right hand is doing, and that's exactly how I've been able to get myself out of countless potentially disastrous situations. That is exactly why I didn't choose to confide in my friend about my plans, I had no worries about him telling Nyla, they barely even interacted with each other, and not at all since Stephie died almost a year ago. As my mind went back to Stephie, I forced myself to think about other things. Stephie's death took a toll on me harder than it should have, for her just being my friend's wife. There are nights I still wake up from dreams I have about her. I had no idea we had already gotten into the car, but somehow I was home.

"You can go get your car from the parking lot tomorrow I'll make sure nothing happens to it, but you wouldn't even know where to find the key hole much less drive yourself home"

"Yea, alright, well I'll give you a call tomorrow then"

"Good night old friend"

I chuckled at his choice of words before answering. "Nah, not old yet! But I'll see you around Mason, and good night!"

I shut the door and turned to go into the door when I heard his car speed off.

Chapter four Nyla

I heard the alarm go off and wrapped myself in the blankets with the pillow covering my face. I was hoping that Anias would just go to bed without bothering me. For the last couple of hours, I was at home alone just thinking. I want so badly to just move on from this chapter of my life that I feel I am willing to do anything just to turn the page! I quieted my breathing when I heard footsteps coming down the hall way, but for some reason I just couldn't get my heart to stop beating drums in my chest, it wasn't the excitement and anxiousness that I would've felt two years ago when I just married Anias, it was the dread that I felt from the thought of him actually seeking an audience with me. My bedroom door opened allowing the lights from the hall to peek in and I almost released a loud groan when Anias started moving closer into the room. I never did like playing hide and go seek as a child, the thought of getting caught always scared me and caused me to give myself up! The bed sunk as I realized he must have sat down. For what seemed like eternity he did not say a word! Anxiety threatened to overcome me and just before I couldn't take the suspense anymore and was about to 'wake up' per say Anias started shaking me at the shoulders.

"What Anias! For crying out loud I was sleeping!"

"Why are you sleeping in here?"

"What do you mean?" I asked releasing a frustrated sigh. I knew exactly what he meant however I didn't feel like acknowledging his foolery at this moment.

"Nyla! I thought I told you, that you will no longer be sleeping anywhere but or matrimonial bed! Why do you insist on annoying the fuck out of me woman!" I knew he must have been drunk, he never could handle his liquor and when he gets that way he tends to be overly loud, use profanities and become abusive. I wasn't in the mood for all of that tonight, so I decided to take one for the team and gather my things to go to our bedroom, currently I was in one of the guest bedrooms.

"OK Anias, I'm going!"

Anias stayed on my heels the whole way to our bedroom, which was at least three rooms down from the one I was in, this house has five bedrooms and four bathrooms, which were all a waste because we never had guests over. When we got to the room Anias spun me around causing me to drop my phone from my hand, as I bent to pick it up he applied pressure to my shoulders making me fall to my knees.

"Anias what is wrong with you!"

"Stay where you are, it's been quite a while since I had the pleasure of feeling those lips around my dick!" He had a smirk on his face that I wished I could knock right off, knowing Anias though he would slap me right back!

"Anias, you can't seriously expect me to suck your dick after you've been out all day!" That shit just seemed so nasty to me.

"What did I tell you about using that type of language! You are a lady and my wife at that, leave all that street bullshit in the slums where I got you from!" He yelled with specks of spit flying from his mouth, I prayed none of it caught me, I had a phobia for those types of bodily fluids. Anias released himself from his pants through his zippers and just stood there waiting for me to suck his dirty dick. I slowly took him inside my mouth, all the time debating the pros and cons of just biting his whole damn dick of! Shit tasted like salt and piss! And don't ask me how I know what piss tastes like, I just know! I removed my mind from the task at hand and started plotting on my escape.....I had no idea how I was going to get away from him with this dark cloud hanging over my head. But fuck it I was going to die trying!

Chapter five Nyla

For the past three weeks Mason and I have been meeting only once a week, usually, we would see each other at least five times a week only staying away when Anias was home, which was very rarely given his job as a doctor, Anias was a private mental health doctor who owned a pharmacy, attached to his private establishment, that was where I got my first and last job, working as a pharmacy tech. That job didn't last for more than three months however before tragedy struck. Any other day I would have been meeting Mason at the hotel we frequented because if its anonymity, it allowed us to pay in cash and was not very big on identification. If you looked like an adult and had your money, you could get a room. However today just like I've been doing for the last three weeks, I drove to the mall, parked my car, went inside and then slipped around through the back entrance wearing a different blouse and a hat from what I went inside wearing. It was a rather tedious task, but necessary since apparently Anias has been suspecting foul play, Mason wasn't sure if he would have anyone tailing me or not and he wasn't willing to take the chance, hell neither was I ! I got into Masons car and reached over to kiss him on his cheek, however he turned away, deflecting my advances.

"What's the matter with you Mason?"

"Nothing"

"Cut the bullshit! I know when you're in your feelings about something, so just spit that shit out already!" This is what I adore about being with Mason, I was always able to just be myself, if I had spoken like that to Anias, he would have slapped the shit out of me. Without looking at me, Mason answered "I'm sick of this shit Nyla, I am too damn grown to be sneaking around with another man's wife! I'm getting tired of this entire situation! I'm telling you right now, you gotta make a decision you either leave that nigga, or you leave me, because the way I see it your confused ass is getting the best of both fucking worlds!" He yelled hitting the steering wheel in the process. I hate when Mason yells at me, but I would never let him know it.

"Mason I'm try-"

"Man, just shut the fuck up with that bullshit alright! I don't wanna hear that shit, it's been 6 fucking months! You claim you love me and wanna get away from that nigga, but I don't see you doing shit about it!"

"But-"

"But nothing Nyla! You know what just shut the fuck up alright!"

I sat back in my seat and turned my head to the window to keep him from seeing the tears that spilled from my eye, as I discreetly rushed to get rid of them. Only Mason had the ability to hurt me with words, even Anias never could. The drive for the rest of the way was silent before Mason spoke to tell me he was going out of town for a couple of days.

"Well how long is a couple of days?"

"Two, maybe three, I need some time to think about things, plus my family down in Miami has been begging me to come for the longest"

I didn't know what to say about that, I had no right to be mad or even salty, but somehow I was, I was upset that he was leaving town, and going so far away, and I was even more upset that I couldn't go! I would have no excuse to give to Anias, I didn't realize until now how small and practically nonexistent my life was outside of Anias! I wanted to beg him to stay, but I knew he was in his feelings at the moment, so it wouldn't do any good.

***

My meeting with Mason was a complete disaster and for the first time I left feeling completely bummed! All I wanted to do was get to the house and curl up under my sheets, I just did not want to be bothered! When I returned to the mall, it was only three in the afternoon, usually I wouldn't get back until around six, but seeing as Mason and I weren't really feeling each other now, there was no reason to stay that long. As I drove out of the mall parking lot, I could have sworn I saw a car pull out immediately after I did, I watched the car from my rearview mirror it followed me until we got to the intersection on 23rd street, before it veered off. Convinced it was my guilty conscience playing tricks on me I relaxed and continued to drive home. Once I got inside the house I took a cold shower to wash the stickiness of the sweltering day off me and walked into my bedroom, I immediately turned around and sprinted back to the bathroom as I felt something rise from my stomach to my throat! I emptied the contents of my stomach inside the toilet and got up to rinse my mouth, for the rest of the day throughout the night the nausea continued. I told myself and Anias that it must have been something I ate. However, after three days of the persistent vomiting and lightheadedness I was forced to come to terms with the fact that there may be something else wrong with me.

Mason had decided to extend his stay in Miami to another two weeks or so and I was royally pissed that he would be do fucking selfish! I mean he knew how much I needed him here, when we texted last time he gave me another ultimatum, him or Anias, it was easy to choose, but not so easy to act. I bought myself ten pregnancy tests of various brands, I planned on taking all ten of them just to be sure, I had no intentions on going to the doctor because Anias was bound to find out if I did. After seeing ten positive pregnancy tests I had come to terms with the fact I was about to be a mother, my only problem now was figuring out who was the father! I had been slacking on taking my pills lately and I wasn't quite certain if I had taken them the night Anias and I had had sex, come to think of it, I wasn't even certain how far along I was! I really wasn't prepared for this bullshit!

Anias

I had hired a private investigator to follow Nyla for the past four weeks, only that son of a bitch came up empty handed! He claimed she only left the house once per week and when she did she spent the entire day at the mall. At first I was inclined to believe that there was nothing going on with that bitch, but I just couldn't shake the feeling! Nyla didn't have any friends, she was a loner, so it was easy for me to believe she never really left the house, so I called off the investigation despite that voice in my head that told me something was amiss. Imagine my surprise when I came home from work early one afternoon four days ago and saw her getting ready to leave the house. Nothing that I did or said could convince her to stay and I was curious to find out what was so important that she couldn't reschedule. When she got up and left the room to go use the bathroom, I heard something vibrating on the wooden bedside table, realizing it was her phone I picked it up but couldn't gain access to it because I didn't know her code. The message preview that popped up on the screen however was enough for me to know that that bitch was indeed up to no good. The message was from an unknown number telling her to hurry up and that they would be waiting over at the gas station when she got there, instead of the usual spot. I wanted to knock her ass out when she came out of the bathroom but decided to keep my cool until I got some more information, when we arrived at the mall, Nyla exited her vehicle and entered the busy mall, I followed suit, making certain to keep a good amount of distance between us and blend in with the crowd. Nyla disappeared to go into the

Victoria's secret store and I decided to stay outside and watched the door for her, I was there for at least fifteen minutes when I decided to go inside to look for her, after about five minutes of looking around, I concluded that I must have missed her, but I had no idea how! I was watching that door like a hawk! Not to be dissuaded I decided to go to the gas station where the anonymous text said she should go, I went back outside and was thrown off by her car still being in the drive way and became pissed when she was nowhere in sight at the gas station! However, something else caught my eye, I saw Mason get out of his vehicle to pump gas, any other time it wouldn't have been weird to see him there but given the situation at hand my suspicions were heightened. I decided to give him a call to test out my rather farfetched but somewhat plausible theory. I asked my old friend

155

where he was, suggesting that we meet up for a drink, he replied that he was out of town, before pulling off from the gas station. Given the blatant lie he just told, I opted to follow him, and after driving for almost an hour, I saw him exit his vehicle, with my wife in tow! Wearing a completely different outfit from the one she left the house in. The feeling of rage I felt was indescribable as I witnessed my wife and my best friend entering a hotel together. I started off following them, but decided against it, I had to move with some sort of common sense. No need to get caught up in this mess, I was gonna handle it, but on my terms. I went back to the mall and waited until Nyla got back, before pulling off with her. These past four days have been nothing but agony as I drunk myself to oblivion and thought about the deceit that my wife and friend had committed. I had a plan, the perfect one at that, but it would have to wait until my dear friend got back in town, turns out he had left after all.

Chapter 6 Mason

It's been three weeks since I'd been in Miami. As much as I wanted to be back home I must admit the new and fresh scenery did a lot to calm my nerves and give me a new perspective on life. It's been one month less than a year since my wife Sophie died. Sophie was the love of my life, there was nothing too good for me to do for her. She made me smile even through the hardest times and always kept me level headed. I loved Sophie right up until the day she died, but it was as if that loved was corrupted the moment I went home and found her sitting in the bath tub looking pale and most definitely lifeless. I looked around for our son, that was supposed to be with her but there was no sight of him, instead I found a letter. That letter would change my life in a way that I could never even consider. My wife not only took herself away from me, but also our son, my heart, and for a moment my sanity, I sat with her in that bathroom for hours trying to make sense of the two-page letter that was in my hands. My wife had committed suicide because she could no longer live with the heinous decisions she had made in her life. I was angry to the point where I wish I could just wake her lying, conniving, cowardly, selfish bitch ass up and beat her back to death. After barely gathering myself I made the call to the police station and went through the motions in a daze as the officers asked me questions after questions. I made the calls to her family and sat through the funeral days later still in that dazed state of mind, nothing but the words on that paper registered to me.

Not even when the coroners ruled her death an accident by overdose. I received a generous amount of money from her life insurance, and made sure Trent would be taken care of, and have a trust fund to at least get him through college, the remainder went to her funeral and any other expenses we may have had. I never kept a penny of it. Only a month or two after that I set my plans in motion to exact revenge, the dead may not be able to feel anything, but the living sure could and I was gonna make sure he did. I only hope that bitch was looking up from hell and seeing this shit! Deception is always a hard pill to swallow, and I found that shit out the hard way. The only thing is, when I started out on my quest for revenge, I had no idea I was ever going to trip and fall in love again the way I did. That was never on my agenda, now this situation with Nyla had me all fucked up in the head, unsure of how to play my cards, it's a shame she had to get caught in the web of lies that we've created, however her part in this cannot go unclaimed. She knew just like I did the consequences of our actions, the only difference is I knew a little more than she did. When all is said and done however I just hope and pray we can get pass this, before this if anyone had said I would love a woman other than Sophie, I would've called them a fucking liar! My phone rang and I answered it prepared to tell Nyla I was on my way home, I was finally ready to end this little game once and for all, it was time to finally let the cat out of the bag I don't know what Anias' bitch ass has on her but that shit was gonna have to take a back seat to the bone I had to pick with her husband.

" Wassup?"

"Ahhhhhhhhh!!!!!" I quickly took the phone from my ears after hearing Nyla screaming. What the fuck was going on? I asked myself, I was sitting in the airport after my flight home waiting for my Uber to come get me.

"Stop, Anias! Stop!"

"Bitch, shut the fuck up! You and that bitch Mason thought you could get one over on me huh! I'm gonna kill your whore ass and leave you stinking in a ditch somewhere! Bitch I told you, it was till death do us part!"

My blood ran cold, and I sat frozen to my seat as I heard yet another scream from the love of my life. Knowing I was too far away to stop it, I quickly made a call to the police hoping they would at least be able to get there sooner than I could. No way was I allowing Anias to take yet another woman I loved from me!

Chapter 7 Anias

I don't know how it even got to this point. I've been sitting in this chair ....in this house, for the past three hours and 15 minutes, just mentally replaying all the events that took place these past two months. In a very short time my life has changed. I feel like I've been falling for months and I'm finally seeing the ground, I'm finally about to drop. The sad thing is, I'm not so sure if I want to or not. Lifting my head, I look at my wife, her eyes are swollen and blood shot, the tears that spill from them should have moved me but, they didn't. She harbors many emotions that shine through her eyes, among them though the most dominant ones are hurt, guilt, fear, and perhaps a little regret. After all these months, scratch that, after all these years! All these mother fucking years! It figures! Right up until the time I left her this morning, all I saw when I looked in her eyes was the reflection of my own discontent. We've long fallen into an eerie silence, drowning in the abysmal failure of a marriage some would say was doomed from the very beginning. Obsession is something that can cause anyone to make even the craziest decisions. I know now what I had not known then, the feeling I harbored for my wife had absolutely nothing to do with love, it was all just an obsession! An obsession that even now I can't shake. I look at her all battered and bruised and I still felt that intense and uncontrollable urge to possess her! When I found out about her deception it hit me like a huge boulder and sent me into a state of shock and utter denial. I could not believe that something that belonged to me could deceive me in such a way. And the more I thought about the entire situation the livider I became. Mason of all persons! They say karma is a bitch who comes back at you full speed ahead! I guess I didn't know what they meant until now. Almost two years ago I started a dangerous game of deceit and it has finally come back to haunt me. But when I met Sophie, it was imperative that I made her mine, even knowing that she already belonged to my best friend. At first my advances were shot down, Sophie was adamant about her love and loyalty to her husband Mason, I hated the fact that she had rejected me and came up with an idea to get her where I wanted her. One weekend while Mason was out of town on business for his bar I invited myself over to his house, Sophie being the gentle woman she was did

not refuse me entrance to her home, I
brought with me a bottle of Moet, I had
learned that it was her favorite from Mason,
she was reluctant at first, given my previous
attempts to woe her, eventually however I
was able to persuade her to at least take one
drink of the liquor, she did and from there I
knew I had her. Sophie and I had wild
uninhibited sex that night, all over her and
Mason's home, and I was sure had it not
been for the drug she never would have done
anything like that. I chuckled at my own
conning. The next morning, I sent her a
video of our little rendezvous and had her
like putty in my hand. I made her meet with
me whenever I wanted, and not long after
she found out she was pregnant, of course I
was already married to Nyla and was in no
way ready for a child, especially not with
Sophie, but I saw that baby as another way
to have a hold on her. Mason was

completely clueless about what was going on with his wife, he trusted too deeply to ever think there was anything foul going on. I saw the effects of our disloyalty weighing on Sophie, however I was too selfish to care, after the baby was born I demanded a test be done to prove its paternity. The baby turned out to be mine. That I think caused Sophie to go over the edge, she committed suicide not a couple of months later, the funny part is, Sophie died never finding out that I had indeed drugged her, she assumed she had deceived her husband all on her own. When Mason didn't go to get the baby from Sophie's mother I assumed that he was too distraught to take care of the child. I didn't mind though, I never wanted the little bastard in the first place. I look at Nyla cowering in the corner nursing her broken nose, I knew without a doubt that neither of us would be making it out of here alive, so I figured, what was the sense in carry my little secret to the grave.

"You know from the moment I met you I knew I was going to make you mine, but you were just so fucking stuck up I knew I had to come up with a plan to get you off your high horse. Opportunity presented itself that day when I came into the office drunk and ended up giving you the wrong prescription for that patient" before now her head was held firmly between her legs, but it shot up at my revelation. A smirk graced my face at the look of shock and pure hatred that was on hers.

"What are you saying Anias" she asked in a voice above a whisper.

" To be honest it was never my intention to harm that young lady, however I never could control my liquor even though I never wanted to admit it. I came into the office that day under the influence and ended up mixing up the prescription and dosages for two of my patients. I didn't recognize my error until the next morning when she was pronounced dead from a negative reaction to the medication I had you give to her, which stopped her heart." Tears rapidly streamed down her face as she finally realized what I was saying. I was fucked up about the death of that girl, however I saw an opportunity to finally get what I wanted.

"It was you! You killed that girl and ......and....and you blamed it on me! You cruel disgusting son of a bitch! Do you know what I've had to live with these past three years! How could you be so fucking evil!"

Cutthroat Chronicles

"Oh, shut up! What I did saved the both of our asses! Don't think for a minute you would not have gone down with me!"

"How! How Anias! I was only doing my job, I gave out the medication you prescribed! But the prescription showed a different set of pills and dosage from what I gave her-"

"Of course, it did! I snuck into the office after I found out about that girl's death and changed the prescription, so that you would think it was your fault! I needed to have you, and I saw the perfect way! If only you could have kept your legs closed and not be so fucking ungrateful!"

"Ungrateful! You ruined my life! How do you think that by making me think I recklessly killed someone you were helping me!"

"Shut the fuck up!" I yelled feeling as if I was losing the small amount of sanity I was holding on to, this was not the way it was supposed to turn out, I had gotten what I wanted, I should have been happy, but this bitch just had to spoil it!

"Before you married me bitch you were nothing! I made you into something! I took you away from that ghetto lifestyle and made you into a lady! I fucking made you!

" I hate you! You ruined my life! You are a monster! And I regret the day I met your crazy narcissistic ass!" I did it before my mind even registered what I was going to do, I pressed down on the trigger and felt the impact of the gun going off ricochet in my shoulders while the bullet landed in the Nyla's chest I watched as she flew back into the wall and landed on the ground, before I put the gun to my head and pulled the trigger yet again, I faintly saw the silhouette of multiple people bursting through my door and their muffled cries before I closed my eyes and welcomed the darkness that enveloped me.

Epilogue

I rocked back and forth with my baby in my arms as I thought about the chaos my life was, not much more than a year ago. There were days I couldn't believe that all the things that transpired were true, or that I was here, it was nothing short of a miracle! When Anias shot me, I had flatlined twice, on the way to the hospital, and then once more during the surgery to get the bullet - that was swiftly making its way to make heart -out of my body. The doctors thought I wouldn't make it, I was placed in a medically induced coma for three months so that I could recuperate, the doctors said the effort to breathe on my own was taking too big a toll on my body, when I woke up three months later, I was certain there was no way my baby could have made it, but the small round belly I sported said otherwise, I remained in the hospital three more months before the doctors thought I was OK to go home, the entire time I had Mason right by my side. He told me about his wife and the affair she had with Anias, he also confessed that that was the only reason he pursued me, to get back at Anias, I was hurt by his revelation, I felt like everyone around me was only there to deceive me. Speaking of Anias, he had tried to kill himself after he shot me, but the bullet only grazed a part of his cerebrum and damaged it to the point where he was practically a vegetable, he was now in a mental institute where he will be spending the rest of his miserable life. Two months ago, I gave birth to me and Mason's baby destiny, Mason and I weren't together, although I still loved him I needed him to prove to me that I could trust him before I let him back into my life like that. This whole situation with Anias has me not even trusting my own fucking shadow! But I have everything in the world to be grateful for, I am alive, and healthy and gave birth to an equally healthy baby girl, even though she will always have some breathing problems due to the slight underdevelopment of one or her lungs, she is more than fortunate to be here. Maybe one day I will find it in myself to forgive Anias for what he did and tried to do to me, but for now I'm content in knowing that he will never be able to harm another person again. They say revenge is a dish best served cold, and karma is the baddest bitch around, and guess what! I believe them!

Mambo Papissa

By: Elise Lang

Dozens of red robes lined the corridor all worn by men, except her own. The last woman that stood in this position had been tied to a horse ,dragged through the city and stoned. Yet here she was skin, and eyes as richly colored as maple syrup, ivory streaked hair pinned neatly under a biretta and a face free of any signs of age or consternation. Though she felt none on this day Jeanne Cassard was no stranger to angst, she'd grown up in Haiti during a time where there was no such thing as middle class you were either rich or poor. As a girl both her mother and father Worked tirelessly to put her through the esteemed Lady of The Cross Academy. Her parents took little to no pay from the school in exchange for her tuition. they knew the sacrifice was necessary after hearing Pope John Paul admonish Haitian society for its inequality during his 1983

tour of Central America . Though Johanne
was an intellectual match for any child born
into better circumstances ,they still evoked
the powers of the loa to ensure her
acceptance and equal treatment at the
affluent school attended by the President's
daughter and the French Prime Minister's
son. Jeanne recalled a close friendship with
both Narcisse Chopard and Celestine
Duvalier she'd grown so close to them in
fact by their last term at Lady of the cross
she knew their greatest desires. Narcisse
wanted to become the Pope and Celestine
wanted to become the Wife of Narcisse
Chopard. Jeanne simply wanted to attend
the university in Port Au Prince, Hers

seemed to be the only goal that was realistic

. She often wondered if her mother being the

Great Mambo Claudette Cassard made her

humble ambitions more attainable. Until one

day she allowed her curiosity to garner the

best of her and she took both Narcisse and

Celestine to the humble dwelling that

housed her mother and father. Claudette was

a knowing woman, she knew why her child

was there with the boy that had been

harmed by a priest at his school in France

causing his father to ship him to Haiti

before a scandal erupted , and the girl that

was so blindly in love with the boy that she

could not see his disinterest in her. Claudette

chanted under her breath until the three

young people in her kitchen were silenced by a clap of thunder. Jeanne was in awe as she heard her mother faintly chanting vre dezi the chant of true desire. The atmosphere crackled with palpable power before the cottage door was pushed open by a hurricane force wind and the lights flickered before shrouding them in darkness. Claudette quickly lit three candles she kept on hand especially for Sevis Lwa. She then gave a candle to each of them and without verbal invitation, three loa visible only to Claudette, entered the dwelling. Jeanne could feel their presence she'd witnessed evocations many times. Though she couldn't see them Jeanne was certain they were here in the form of their catholic

syncretic counterparts . Undoubtedly she

was correct, Erzulie Dantor in the form of

St. Jeanne d'arc blew out the pink candle

she was holding. Baron Samedi in the form

of his familiar St. Expedite blew out the red

candle held by Narcisse, and his wife

Maman Brigitte disguised as St. Brigid

extinguished the flame of the white candle

held by Celestine. Then the rain ceased the

winds calmed to a whisper and the

electricity returned. there was no flailing or

convulsing involved in this mounting she

had simply given them the power to

manifest their deepest most repressed

desires. As the three of them walked back to

their dormitories Narcisse was the first to
feel an overwhelming since of longing he
looked at Jeanne in that moment knowing
that she was the answer to his prayers. He no
longer needed to lead a life of piety to
remove the shame left from his childhood,
he only needed Jeanne. Jeanne could feel
Narcisse watching her as she comforted
Celestine who'd been sulking the entire
walk . He was too consumed with his own
yearnings to empathize with her. After what
happened to him as a boy and many years of
internal conflict this feeling was something
he had to act on immediately. Once
Celestine went into the room she shared
with the second-year daughter of her father's

personal secretary. He grabbed Jeanne before she could go into her room and kissed her she was speechless. Jeanne was unable to resist Narcisse while under the influence of Ezrulie . He took her there in the corridor and she said nothing knowing what her mother had done. Narcisse was beyond consolation as he broke down sobbing tears of relief and guilt . He was free from the scars of his childhood, yet he'd hurt the person he desired above all else. The last term passed, and Jeanne avoided both Narcisse and Celestine. In all honesty she avoided everyone as she felt the child of Narcisse Chopard growing in her belly. Claudette knew the truth she'd created it.

This was all her doing . Jeanne had some idea but until she came to her mother with her own truth Claudette would be tight lipped as well. The wait was not very long Jeanne sat down with her mother within the month agreeing that the child should be born in neighboring Puerto Rico to secure a U.S. citizenship. Jeanne as always followed her mother's every instruction. Even after the incident with Narcisse she still trusted her judgement. The day Jeanne gave birth she realized once and for all that her mother was not acting in her best interest. After expressing her wishes not to see Narcisse she was shocked to see him walk into her hospital room with Celestine. What's more she was shocked when without a word they

walked out with her son in his arms. Once

again she found herself unable to speak,

unable to defend herself against him she

knew the Loa were working because she

was powerless to do anything but cry.

Narcisse could hear her sobbing as he took

his son from the one that he loved, the

woman whose rejection of him had hurt him

so deeply he was now hardened to her. How

could she deny him the right to know he had

a son? Celestine tried to comfort Narcisse by

reminding her husband that she could never

have children she also reminded him that

Claudette Cossard had informed them that

Jeanne intended to give the child up for

adoption to a family in the U.S.. She convinced him they were doing what was best as he would be continuing his education in the States and his son would have a better life with them than strangers. Jeanne swore that day that she would be Vindicated. That was 33 years ago, 33 years of concealing her sex and her identity. Spending the first 15 of those years perfecting her role as father Jean Cassard and the last 18 rising through the clerical hierarchy to her current position of Cardinal. This day her vindication would be made absolute. As the White smoke filled Vatican City and the news of the first Haitian Pope was announced. The President of France felt a great sense of pride for himself having grown into manhood in Haiti and a greater sense of pride for his son who was half Haitian. Narcisse was even more filled with pride when the papal secretary called his hotel the following evening offering him a private audience with the pope. Narcisse felt a sense of anxiety as he walked into the inner most chambers of the Vatican. Immediately he was struck by the same lust he felt more than 30 years ago in Haiti a desire he hadn't felt for his wife Celestine or any other woman since his son's mother rest her soul she'd died in the earthquake in Haiti seven years earlier . He felt disgusted and repulsed as he gazed upon the man cloaked in White from crown to sole. Narcisse felt those same conflicted emotions he experienced in his childhood returning. He felt as if he wanted to vomit as he kneeled to kiss the ring of the Pontiff. Jeanne was amused knowing Narcisse thought he was in love with a man. Although it was a cruel game she had chosen to play it was her mother's spirit that lived on through her after her passing in the Haitian earthquake of 2010 that caused her to find amusement at the expense of the privileged. Narcisse had taken her heart when he took their son from her and now she would take his every thought

The Serpent

By: Quiana Golde

Snakes were supposed to be reptiles not

people

I'm feeling like Eve in the Garden of Eden

Ate from the tree that knew good and evil

All because of THE SERPENT

She was certain THE SERPENT was

looking out for her

Because he was persuasive when he lied to

her

Just the way you're lying to me now Sir

You think I can't just get another?

Nobody like you, you say? Honey I want

better.

Maybe it's my fault, I shouldn't have

introduced her to you

Then again why was it her you chose to

pursue?

An Anthology of Deception

You made me look a fool one too many

times

She was my best friend - Now you're both

telling me lies

I'm done, not listening to none of ya'll cries

Face the consequences of your crimes

I wasn't enough, so you got another?

Little dick nigga, I'm glad I fucked your

brother.

Peace.

Mask Deception

By: El Nino The Prince

An Anthology of Deception

#MaskDeception
How could you sit there & lie to a G/
Talking bout you love me?
Mom died , I cried/
Where we're ü , Justin Bieber sing.
Where were you when 3y3 needed Ü
/ No where to be seen.
3y3 should expose you
for your fraudulence/
I don't have to do a thing.
Dj Khaled voice/
#CongratulationsYouPlayedYourself .
Thanks for playing/ leave.
Some been gone for the longest/
Won't even check in to see.
thought we had something real/
I guess it's plain to see.
You're the reason we're distant/
Don't "#HeyStranger✋ " me.

Men like, women lie /
Time reveals everything.
Actions speak louder than words/
Silence says everything.
Love is an action word/
Show it better than you tell it chief.
Real don't just recognize real/
Real recognize everything.
They don't know how real
you kept it with them /
til the day you leave.
Pulled a Drake on that ass/
Nothing was the same, sheesh.
Don't fall for the fake love/
Another prey of deceit.
Love is blind /
When it takes over
It gets harder to see.
There's a thin line between
love and hate my Gs /
God is love,
Hate can only enter the weak.
Sometimes
hate comes dressed As love/
Trust your instincts B.
Something don't seem right/
Everything ain't as it seems.
I can feel it in the air /
Beanie siegal warning.
There's wisdom in being dumb/
Gotta question everything.

An Anthology of Deception

Sometimes you gotta play the fool/
Being too smart can kill you chief.
Don't be so playa that you forget
You're still a piece/
Everyone ain't playing games,
Don't get caught slippin my liege.
Make ya next move ya best move/
That was the wrong move, R.I.P.
You're a dead man walking/
Some are alive
but they're dead to me.
#LiveÑLetDie /
In our past life they're buried.
Sometimes #ExMarksTheSpot /
There lies our treasured memories.
Leave the past in the past/
Sometimes it haunts us , relentlessly.
Some are still slaves to past hurt/
To them the future's too dark to see
Hearts left in bankruptcy
Due to past philanthropy/
#CounterfeitLove💔
From the fakes who can't keep it real, leave.
Hearts don't always break even/
But we get even , eventually.
#SincerelyYoursElNinõThePrince /
What goes around comes around, si

Like A Good Neighbor

By: Free-Flo

195

Everyone wants to have a good neighbor, right?

Damian and Laurel, both 28, had been together almost 5 years. They lived in the Hardy Trails Townhomes located in Atlanta, Georgia. They had lived in that townhome community for three of the years that they'd been together. They had a 4-year-old daughter together, Mila, who they created after being together only a month. Even though it was only supposed to be a one-night stand, they somehow fell for one another.

Damian was African American and Laurel was Caucasian. Their families didn't approve of them being together yet that didn't stop them. Their townhome community was very diverse. Their downstairs neighbor, Marisol, was a 45-year-old Hispanic/African American widowed woman who lived alone. She had no kids but always talked to the kids that lived nearby and had snacks for them all. Then there was Mr. and Mrs. Chung, the couple who lived across from Marisol and owned several convenience stores in the area. Next door to Damian and Laurel was Kartez, 27, and Melissa, 25, an African American couple with 5-year-old twin girls.

Everyone pretty much looked out for one another, which was the way neighbors should be. The younger couples who lived upstairs would argue from time to time but everyone minded their own business. Kartez and Melissa always had arguments that everyone could hear but it never got physical. Mr. and Mrs. Chung tried to give both couples advice any chance they could. They were 60-something year old couple who had been together for over 20 years.

One day, Damian walked came home and was about to give Laurel a kiss but she jumped and hurriedly closed her computer.

He had never seen her so jumpy so he asked her what was wrong.

"What's up babe? What you all jumpy for?" he asked, thinking it had to be nothing because he trusted her. She'd never given him a reason to think otherwise.

"Babe, you know I can't lie to you. We need to talk," she sighed, then lowered her head as if she was ashamed.

He sat down and allowed her to explain. Evidently, two weeks before their one-night stand, she'd had another one-night stand with another guy she had known for a while. She explained to Damian that the guy had messaged her on The Book and told her he felt that Mila was his daughter and not Damian's. He threatened to tell Damian if she didn't allow him to take a test and be sure. Damian looked confused but then shrugged his shoulders.

"It really doesn't matter what dude is talking about because I know that's my daughter. She is mixed and there's no way she could be for anyone else because I'm the only black guy you have ever been with. Give me this computer so I can set dude straight," he said, snatching the laptop out of her hand.

She was about to say something but Damian had already opened the computer and was about to type a reply to the guy, Marcus, but stopped dead in his tracks when he saw the profile pic. Marcus was a black guy. *"Why would she lie about being with black guys?"* he thought to himself as he began to read all of Marcus' messages. Marcus was going off in his messages about Laurel sleeping with several black guys in his neighborhood back then and how he knew that had to be his child because of the timing. According to Marcus' timeline, Mila was born right on time. Laurel had told Damian she went into labor two weeks earlier than she was supposed to due to stress. He never questioned her until now.

"Why the hell would you lie about fucking black dudes? I really don't understand! 7 years! 7 YEARS! And you didn't think to tell me not one time that it was a possibility that Mila wasn't mine?

Come on man, that's my baby, man! No, God, no. This can't be happening to me," Damian said through his tears.

"I'm so sorry. I knew he was no good and you were a nice guy and I know that doesn't make it right but I knew you'd be a better father. Baby, I am so sorry, come here so I can......," she said, trying to grab his hand. He slapped her hand away.

"GET THE FUCK OFF OF ME! Don't say shit to me! I can't even look at your ass right now. I'm about to grab some clothes and go to my brother's house for a few days. Don't contact me at all!" Damian shouted. He went into the room, packed enough clothes for more than just 'a few days', and walked out the door, slamming it on his way out.

Mila was on the playground with Kartez's daughters and although she tried to get her dad's attention to say bye and give him a hug, Damian was too pissed to even notice. He sped off while burning rubber. Marisol heard the tires and walked outside just as a crying Laurel was running down the stairs to try to catch Damian.

"What's wrong sweetheart?" asked Marisol.

Laurel couldn't even speak. She collapsed into Marisol's arms and cried uncontrollably for over ten minutes. Once Laurel could calm down, she explained everything to Marisol. Marisol was speechless.

"I don't know what to say sweetheart. I can't imagine how either of you must be feeling right now. Is there anything I can do?" Marisol asked.

"You know I work the night shift 4 days a week and he works the day shift Monday through Friday. He usually picks her up from school and helps her with homework and gets her ready for bed since I don't get off from work until 8-9 pm. I know this is a lot to ask, but could you watch her for me this week? That will at least give Damian time to cool down," Laurel begged.

"I have no problem doing that for you baby. You know I love all these kids. Just give me the details tomorrow and starting Monday, I will begin picking her up if you need me to. And just a bit of advice, don't bother Damian. He is a man and his pride is hurting right now so just give him some time," and with that Marisol patted Laurel on the back and went inside.

That following week, Marisol began picking Mila up from school. She helped her with her homework and they even played games and did girly things like polishing their nails and toes. Mila was having the time of her life.

"I wish my mom would do things like this with me. My dad polishes my nails and toes sometimes but it seems more fun with just the girls," Mila said with a giggle.

Her comment made Marisol's eyes tear up. Her heart had yearned for a child for years. After so many miscarriages, she had given up. '*Maybe once my adoption paperwork goes through, I will be able to adopt a little girl of my own and do these types of things all the time,'* she thought to herself. One week turned into two, then three. Soon, it had been over a month since Damian had left and Marisol took over. One day, the school called Laurel to tell her that Mila wasn't at school that day.

"That can't be true. I dropped her off this morning myself," she explained to the principal.

"Did you see her go into the building?" the principal asked.

"No ma'am, I didn't. I looked down because I dropped my cell phone and when I looked up, she was gone. I assumed she had run into the building with the car rider monitor," Laurel said through a panic.

"Oh my God, need to notify the police. Hold on," said the principal.

The principal called the police on three-way with Laurel on the phone. They filed a report and the search began. They asked several questions to the school, Laurel, Damian, and even the neighbors. One of the neighbors had to have exposed the big secret about Mila's real father because they showed up to ask Laurel more questions. She told them everything that she thought would help but couldn't figure out why it mattered.

The next day, she was notified that Damian was a person of interest. She didn't believe that he would ever do anything to Mila. When she went with Marisol to see him in court, the cold look he gave her made her think otherwise. She first thought he looked at her with disgust because of what she had done, but Marisol had convinced her that his look was a guilty look. She said he probably couldn't handle the betrayal and did the unthinkable.

Three more weeks went on and still no Mila. One day, a little girl's body was found in a lake nearby. Laurel just knew it had to be Mila. She hated herself for lying to Damian and now felt even more guilt because she had lost her little girl. The cops said the little girl resembled Mila but they would need her to come down to the morgue and confirm. Laurel asked Marisol to take her since couldn't handle the task alone.

Marisol dressed herself and walked into Laurel's apartment 30 minutes later. She called out to her but there was no answer.

Once she made her way to the kitchen, she made a horrifying discovery. Laurel had slit both her wrists and was near death on the kitchen floor. Marisol called 911 but by the time they made it to the hospital, she was pronounced dead. Not even an hour after, the news released information that the deceased little girl wasn't Mila after all. With no body and Laurel's suicide, Damian was still charged with kidnapping Mila. The prosecutor wanted to stick him with murder charges since everyone assumed that Mila had to be dead by now. Detectives tried to question Damian over and over but got the same response.

"I already told ya'll! Yes, I found out she wasn't my daughter and yes, I was pissed at her mom. But I would have never hurt my baby girl! I don't care what that dude said, that is MY baby! I just needed some time to cool off and let everything sink in. You have to believe me sir," Damian

205

pleaded over and over. No one believed him though. All signs pointed to him.

The prosecutor could get him charged with kidnapping and 1st degree murder, even without a body. Damian passed out in court when he was read his sentence of life without the option of parole. Even his family had begun to believe he had done it. Not even a week later, Damian hung himself in his cell. People said he probably couldn't handle the consequences of his actions.

Back in Hardy Trails Townhomes, everyone was saying their goodbyes to Marisol. They felt for her when she said she needed to get as far away from the drama as she could. She couldn't handle losing her favorite neighbors. The whole thing was a tragedy. They said their goodbyes and everyone went inside. Marisol started her car, took one last look at her old home, and hit the highway.

"So, are you sure my mommy won't be mad that I wanted you to be my new mommy? She's okay with that?" a little voice asked.

"Yes dear, I am absolutely positive. She wanted you to be happy. The place we are going to live is far away and no one knows us there. We are going to play a little game. Instead of being called Mila, your new name will be Leah and mine will be Alma, your adoptive mommy. And you can't tell anyone about your parents because then, that will mess up the whole game. Okay?" Marisol said.

"Yes ma'am, mommy Alma!" Mila giggled.

"Good, now take a nap. It's going to be a long drive," Marisol said, turning up the radio.

As she drove, she hoped like hell Mila would not grow up and question her about her parents or go looking for answers on her own. That would be the day karma came back to bite her in the ass and possibly take her out!

About the Authors

Thornne Xaiviantt

Thornne Xaiviantt was born the youngest of three children in Columbus, Ohio. His writing journey began at 9 years old which was the beginning of his now 31 years of experience. He has had freelance poetry and anthology projects published and one co-authored book. These works include the co-authored book, *A Soldier's Promise,* in 2012 and anthology appearances in *Healing Through Words* and *Gathering of Words* (Inner child Press), *Erotic Tranquility Volumes 1 and 2* (Steamy Trails LLC), and *Poetic Lounge Volume 1.*

El Niño The Prince

What began as a recreational/ therapeutic
process soon became
a spiritual calling for New Jersey native Robert
Lee Austin III, artistically known as El Niño the
Prince.
His presence and poetry are affirmations of
resilience, and Universal healing on Divine
levels.
El Niño started writing to battle
his personal bouts of depression as a means to
declutter an overactive mind.
He soon realized that more than this, it became a
portal of connection to other like-minded souls
fighting similar battles when he decided to start
sharing them via Instagram with his followers
who resonated with struggle.
Inspiring other artists and people to embrace
their gifts and remind them of the greatest
reflection within themselves helped create
perspectives that they may or may not have been
ignorant to.
Hence his debut work, the E-Book, *'Reflections
of a Broken Mirror'*, which puts a poetical and
satirical spin on real life battles and phases we
all go through finding ourselves
(Available through Amazon and Kindle
marketplace).
Be sure to follow his social media to stay
updated on this soothsaying Wordsmith!
Instagram: @Elninotheprince Facebook: Robert
El Niño the Prince Austin

Elise Lang

Shannon Elise Lang is a Baton Rouge, Louisiana native that's new to the world of writing. Fiction writing is a long-treasured hobby of Elise's. It is a hobby that she nearly gave up after experiencing a devastating setback in her writing when the hard drive containing all her work was damaged during the Great Louisiana flood of 2016. A discouraged Elise took what she thought would be an indefinite break from writing, but with the encouragement of her brother, Elise's interest in writing returned. Elise also attributes much of her inspiration to write again to reading the novel *Shoulda Just Killed Me* by author and mentor, Florencia "Free-Flo" Freeman. Coming out of her hiatus from writing, Lang stated, "Holding a hard copy of published work written by someone I'd known since childhood ignited something in me. It was a powerful motivational tool. I don't see myself ever giving up again because something I write could inspire someone to pursue their dreams as well."

Quiana Golde

Quiana Golde is an author who writes young adult and urban fiction novels. Informally, she had been writing for four years before she became a published author. To date, Quiana Golde has 5 published books and her first novel, *Soul Attraction*, made it to number 7 on the Amazon Best Seller's list. She is presently working on more novels for her current and future readers. She was born in Jamaica and has several hobbies including dancing, cooking and of course, reading and writing.

Hebrew King

HEBREWKING is from Clarksdale, Mississippi and has been writing since 2008. He writes in the genres of spirituality, romance, motivation, creative thinking, pain and love. His hobbies include sharing scriptures daily, playing basketball, working out, writing poetry, being with his son, traveling, training individuals, being one with the wilderness and praising Yahuah.

Monroe Borders

Alice "Monroe Borders" Borders is a girl who grew up in the city of New York, inspired by the different styles of art that stood out to her. She has always loved music but when her mother passed away, she began writing poetry and songs to help with the pain. Now almost two decades later, she has some poetry online and is currently pursuing different avenues to get her work out there to reach others.

Eyeris Morgan

Eyeris Morgan is a New Jersey native with a
thirst for cosmic knowledge and passion for
crystals and creativity.
Where the wolf and the butterfly meet,
Her mind rests in between.
The tension of magnets going the same way
chasing the attraction of human and
karmic lesson: this is her art when in deep
thought.
A woman of few spoken words but various
mental silences that vibrate like clear quartz,
She is a Universal muse.
Her writing speaks of a love she went in debt
giving to others when she could have given it to
herself for free, and her wordplay is nothing
more than self-inflicted wounds that have
become battle scars she earned on the path
to self-love.

Tasheka Peterkin

Tasheka Peterkin is an aspiring 21-year-
old author from the island of Jamaica. From the
tender age of 8, she realized her undying passion
for writing. However, with the lack of
motivation, her passion was placed on the back
burner. In her last year of high school, she
rekindled her dream of becoming an author by
entering the first piece of writing she ever shared
with another person into an island wide creative
writing competition. She was proud of herself

when she was placed fourth in the Island High School section of the competition. Since then, she has been creating pieces that she has kept to herself until now. She intends to use this platform as a way of getting her work out there. God's willing and with a LOT of hard work, she will eventually become a seasoned author and finally fulfill her dreams!

Free-Flo

Free-Flo was born in Lafayette, LA, and raised in both Ville Platte, LA and Baton Rouge, LA. She now resides in League City, TX with her 3 children. Free-Flo is an avid reader and decided to share her love of books with the world because reading and writing are her first loves. Her vivid imagination and creativity motivated her as a young girl to write short stories, music, and poetry which she has continued to do throughout the years. In 2013, she first published novel, *Shoulda Just Killed Me*, a fiction drama.

Her second novel, *Rejection, Revelations, & Reality,* was published in 2017 and is a collection of poetry, songs, and short stories. She was also a part of two anthologies, *I Can Hear Your Heart,* led by author Yara Kaleemah and *The Blackprint,* led by author Hood

Chronicles. She now balances being a mother, school teacher, and writer. Her goals are to engage her readers and hopefully become a best-seller one day. Free-Flo is currently working on her third novel, *So Much For Happy Endings,* which is a sequel to *Shoulda Just Killed Me*. She also plans to begin writing young adult books.